D0940886

HER IRISH FLIRT

O'KEELEY'S IRISH PUB: BOOK 3

PALMER JONES

SWEET BLOOMS PUBLISHING, LLC

Copyright © 2019 by Palmer Jones

All rights reserved.

No part of this book may be reproduced in any form or by any electronic or mechanical means, including information storage and retrieval systems, without written permission from the author, except for the use of brief quotations in a book review.

This is a work of fiction. Names, characters, businesses, places, events, locales, and incidents are either the products of the author's imagination or used in a fictitious manner. Any resemblance to actual persons, living or dead, or actual events is purely coincidental.

Print Edition: 978-1-7333968-5-1

E-Book Edition: 978-1-7333968-4-4

Cover design by JD&J Design.

Editing by Patricia Ogilvie.

First Edition

ALSO BY PALMER JONES

Cathal O'Keeley landed a solid punch square on the jaw of the huge idiot. The impact sent the man stumbling to his knees. Not an easy feat seeing as the man was over six feet five inches. A few inches taller than himself.

But he'd take on a giant if it meant teaching a man a lesson on how to treat a woman.

"What the hell?" Fiona charged through the crowd that had gathered. Her gaze barely skimmed over the dumb man shaking his head, trying to come to his senses kneeling on the floor of her bar.

His fierce Fiona had her dark blue, accusing, fairy eyes leveled at Cathal. They easily showed her emotions.

"That's the fourth time you've laid someone out in my bar."

Cathal flexed his hand. Nothing broken. But it'd be sore in the morning. He didn't have a temper, by rule, more like a minimal ability to watch men lay their hands on a woman in any other way than God intended. The idiot in question had shoved his girlfriend against the wall when she accidentally spilled her drink on him. The accidental part of the equation didn't even matter.

"You need to leave," Fiona said. She tucked a strand of smooth, red hair behind her ear before crossing her arms. "Now, Cathal."

He held up his hands, smiling despite the thump of adrenaline, pushing him to hit the jackass on the floor again.

And again.

He could control it. Or try to. "Fine, Fiona, darling. For you, I'll leave. I know the routine by now." He turned toward the brunette, still hovering in the corner. Crooking his finger, he motioned her closer, but she shook her head.

He sighed. "But do me a favor and make sure she has a ride home." He pulled two twenties from his wallet and passed them to Fiona. "If it's more than that, just add it to my tab."

The firm press of Fiona's unpainted lips softened. Cathal had caught himself on more than one occasion, wondering exactly how they'd feel. It was that obsession that turned what had once been a joke into a necessity, coming back to her bar every Friday or Saturday night—trying his luck again.

Failing again.

"Go," she added a little softer.

The man rose to his full height, touching his jaw and wincing. "I don't know who the hell you think you are, but you aren't going anywhere." He fisted his hands. "I'm not done with you."

Cathal smirked. He'd been called cocky for most of his life, and he assumed the description suited him. "You never even had a chance to start with me." He shook his head to clear the buzz and urge to fight the man, looking back at Fiona. She stepped in between them and in danger. He'd leave if only to make sure she didn't get caught up in the middle of the fight.

Then, he *wouldn't* be able to stop himself.

Giving her a wink to gloss over the anger, he said, "I'm only leaving because you want me to."

She rolled her eyes. "I feel honored." She gave his shoulder a shove toward the door. "I'm sure there are thousands of women in Atlanta who'd clamor for your attention. And then maybe you won't end up with your Irish butt thrown in jail again."

He covered his heart with his hand as he walked backward. "Oh, it sounds like you care."

"I'm tired of bailing your ass out." She waved him away. No smile. No laugh. His Fiona was rock solid in her determination *not* to like him. She never had as far as he knew. For almost nine months, he'd sat at the end of her bar, trying to charm a smile or two from his red-headed beauty and nothing. But he refused to give up.

He started whistling and walked out of the bar and into the early spring air, still trying to swallow down the adrenaline. Seeing a man touch a woman that way, sent his brain into a frenzy. Fiona had probably figured that out after the first time he'd slammed a guy on her bar for grabbing at his sister-in-law, Selena. But it always took a couple hours to level out again.

Bring himself back from the shadows of his memories.

At eleven on a Saturday night, he had several options to consider. Going home was one of them. Ducking into another bar, finding a sweet woman to take his mind off

Fiona and, well, everything really, was another option. With both of his brothers tied down now, he'd found himself sorely lacking male companionship.

Then there was the worse option for a Saturday night. Work. O'Keeley's Irish Pub was nearing closing, and if the lights weren't off and doors locked yet, they would be soon.

He turned right at the crosswalk, away from his office, away from the pub, and toward another loud bar. Surely, he'd find himself a distraction, at least for the night.

The bar met his low expectations. Loud, pulsating music. A press of people at the bar that three bartenders were trying to serve. At one point in his life, he'd have loved the atmosphere. He glanced around, not missing the way a few women watched him.

He wasn't vain, despite how much his family teased him. Being vain meant he agreed with the assessment that he could get any woman he wanted based on his looks. That wasn't true. He'd been shot down before.

Just look at Fiona. She had no problem telling him to get the hell out of her bar. Although, the nine months of rebuffs did hurt a little.

"Hi," a woman yelled. That was necessary as the music was two levels too high, in his opinion.

He smiled and used it as an excuse to bend down closer to her. "Hi."

She pointed at the dance floor, a throng of people pressed up against each other, moving as one mass to the loud techno music.

He wanted a quiet drink at the end of Fiona's bar.

"Do you want to dance?" She smiled up at him, hopeful. Her heart-shaped face was cute. A short, bob of blonde hair ended a little above her shoulders.

He tapped on her beer bottle. "How many of those have

you had?" Because he'd learned that lesson a long time ago when he awoke next to a woman who didn't remember him. In all fairness, he didn't remember her name either, but it'd bothered him.

She wiggled three fingers.

"What's your name?"

"Lena. Yours?"

"Cathal."

"Irish?" She grinned and rolled her eyes at his hesitation. "Sorry, it sounds like you have an accent in here."

"I do." He waited while she took the last drink of her beer and set it on a small table behind her. "Do you want to dance? My friends are completely boring right now." She waved to a group of women who stood in the corner, watching them. They all snapped their heads away when she waved.

He laid an arm over her shoulders. "Come on, Lena, we'll show them what they're missing." And he'll distract himself for the evening.

"If you press charges, then I'll be sure that your girl there presses charges against you." Fiona Grant crossed her arms and stared down the big brute, a little impressed at how hard Cathal hit. The man's girlfriend had taken refuge in Fiona's small office, still shaking and slightly drunk.

"She won't do that." He huffed, pressing the ice bag against his jaw. His girlfriend had said the same thing. She didn't want trouble. Wouldn't leave him no matter what. Fiona hated that, but she wouldn't go completely off the chain like Cathal.

She'd seen the guy push her.

And like Cathal, she sprang into action, ducking underneath the bar, heading in their direction and ready to kick his ass out. But Cathal had beat her there.

"I think that guy that hit me is mental. He looked crazed like he wanted to rip my throat out." The big guy cracked his knuckles. "But he knew I'd kick his ass, that's why he left."

The swelling along the side of the man's face and the gentle way he cupped it made it look as though Cathal had dislocated his jaw with that one punch. And she hated to admit that watching Cathal defend a woman he didn't know, like he'd done the other times, brought a rush of heat to her cheeks.

"My—friend—" that was the only term she knew to use, "—he doesn't like to see women treated that way. It's sorta his trigger, you know." Calling Cathal a friend was a stretch. He'd tried to talk, flirt, charm his way into her life, and she'd resisted. One charming man already made a fool out of her. It wouldn't happen again. It didn't matter how tempting he was in those moments. His eyes. That shit-eating grin. He was a playboy. A flirt. A man who had as many bed partners as she had in variety of liquor behind the bar.

The man stood, handed her the bag of ice, and shook his head. "I'm out of here." He paused by the office door and waited. The woman emerged, her mascara smeared, and her nose red from crying. He put an arm around her shoulder and walked out.

Fiona had drama with her ex-fiancé but nothing like abuse. Their relationship ended over a simple case of cheating. He'd cheated on her the night before her wedding, and she didn't accept his apology.

Fiona snorted and walked back to the bar. That was a joke. He didn't apologize. More like he tried to convince her that she didn't see him having sex with her maid-of-honor in the honeymoon suite. But her mom had seen it even though she denied it later.

Her customers had disappeared with the commotion and subsequent loss of the only bartender...her. She'd close up for the night. No use sitting in an empty bar, burning electricity, and reminiscing over her failed relationship.

The bouncer, Chuck, leaned on the counter, lacking a smile. Typical. "You done for the night?"

"Yeah." She picked up a glass and set it in the washer. "Cathal cleared the bar like usual."

"I don't know why you keep letting him back in. I can deny him entry, you know. Just say the word. I don't like the way he looks."

Of all the things that annoyed her about Cathal, his looks weren't one of them. If she ignored the cocky, arrogant attitude, the man was very nearly perfect. Blue eyes. Light brown hair. A body that looked long and lean under the dress shirts and slacks he wore. Sexy as hell.

But he knew it.

Just like her ex-fiancé, Hugo.

Chuck sighed and stood up. "Whatever. I'm here if you need me." He knocked on the wooden bar top. "I'll see you tomorrow night."

"Bye." She finished cleaning her bar, the thoughts of Cathal still confusing her. He'd hit on her regularly for the past few months, ever since he first rescued his sister-in-law from some perv who'd grabbed her. Nearly killed the man in the process. Fiona's testimony had cleared him of the charges but had earned her a new customer. Same seat. Every week.

Cathal tipped her well enough to cause guilt at her

annoyance with him. It's like his tip was payment for her being subjected to his failed flirting attempts. Some nights, when she was tired, his Irish accent almost made her forget that she didn't want a smooth-talking man ever again.

She sighed and grabbed her purse, flipped off the lights to the bar, and locked the front door. Her car, always parked in the closest spot to the exit, was something she loved. Her BMW. But that brought on another wave of guilt. Her parents owned the car just like they paid for her apartment.

She'd agreed to the conditions of their continued support by ignoring the fact she was supposed to return to Hugo at the end of the separation. They'd never set a time limit. Eventually, her father would come calling for her. Then, she'd cut off all her financial ties with them.

For the time being, it gave her the freedom to reinvest in her bar.

She drove to her apartment, letting the valet take her car before she hauled her tired body through the lobby and up the elevator. She scanned through her email as she walked down the hallway to her apartment door. Like usual, Hugo had emailed her.

She started to delete it without opening it, but their seven years of relationship, even if he did ruin it, made her tap on the email.

Weekly, he demanded a firm date to end their estrangement. She half-laughed.

Separation.

Estrangement.

Those were terms he and her parents put on it. Fiona flat out broke it off. She'd happily give back the apartment and her car if that were necessary to get her parents and Hugo to acknowledge the truth. Everyone kept supporting her, thinking she'd miss that lifestyle and cave in. That would *never* happen. But, for now, she'd accept the support as a sort of compensation for making her go through hell. At least she finally found happiness in owning her own bar.

2

Cathal cracked his eyes, his bedroom a little bleary. The clock confirmed he'd passed out a total of three and a half hours. Not bad. Sleeping never came easy. The whiskey and women helped.

His head hurt almost as much as his hand. The dumbass guy had a jaw as solid as a rock. He opened his hand gingerly, trying to determine if he'd broken anything. He would never regret punching the man, but he might hit a softer target next time.

His mind replayed the vision of the woman being shoved against the wall.

No. No regrets, even if a few bones might be cracked.

Sunday meant he'd roll into O'Keeley's Irish Pub a little later in the afternoon. His brother, Brogan, generally ran the pub, but Cathal had volunteered to go into work on Sundays and give Brogan a day off with Selena, his *very* pregnant sister-in-law.

He rolled his ass out of bed and into the shower. He'd met a woman last night. Lisa...maybe. The scent of her perfume still lingered on his skin, and he wanted it off.

He enjoyed women. It helped to keep his mind occupied away from his past. Too bad, his thoughts had continued to travel toward a certain redhead ever since he'd first laid eyes on her nine months ago. But Fiona didn't want anything to do with him, a fact that drove him back to her bar every weekend.

After his long, hot shower, he stepped out, feeling closer to human again. He put on his suit, a requirement his oldest brother said, and headed into the restaurant.

"Hello, Katie," he called as he stepped through the front door. The scent of cottage pie reminded his stomach that he'd not eaten breakfast or lunch, yet. Katie stood at the hostess podium, her hair, now a platinum shade of blond was up in a high ponytail.

She smiled. "Good morning, Mr. O'Keeley."

"Please." He grimaced at the insinuation that he was like his oldest brother. "I'm not Brogan. Cathal will do. You know that."

She smirked. "I do, but I love watching you cringe."

He chuckled and walked through the restaurant. The pub was the brainchild of Cathal's and his two brothers. Rian was the middle child and the chef, the creativity and fame behind the O'Keeley name. Brogan, the oldest, made it happen. The staffing, scheduling, money, everything that made O'Keeley's run like a greased machine was due entirely to Brogan.

Cathal helped some with the legal side of the business, but there wasn't much else a lawyer could do running a restaurant. His brothers often referred to him as lazy, and maybe he was, but being serious brought out more emotions than he wanted to handle. He saved his "serious" days for the times the law firm called him into work.

"Cathal?" The bartender called his name. He turned,

spotting a pretty woman that seemed familiar. She tilted her head to the side as he tried to place her face. "Do you remember me?"

He grinned, something he hoped was charming and would earn him an apology as he couldn't remember her. "Give me a hint."

She shook her head. "I wouldn't expect you to remember me, I guess. You're like the dentist."

"That's a new one." He walked to the bar, setting his hands on the beautiful wood they had shipped from Ireland. It was smooth and always felt warm under his hands. Like it was still alive. "How am I like a dentist?"

"You know your dentist's name, right? Well, he has hundreds of patients, so he might not remember you."

Controlling his expression, he ran through a mental list of the women he'd slept with. He would remember that face. Her skin a deep tan, but nothing that gave away her ethnicity. Maybe Egyptian. And now she worked for them. Damn, but Brogan would have his ass for this. His strict no dating policy was fine by Cathal, but surely it couldn't extend to a woman he'd obviously been with *before* they hired her.

"You're a beautiful woman, but I'm afraid—"

She laughed, interrupting his sentence. "I'm Kami Taylor. Or actually Dawson now. You helped me through my divorce." Her brown eyes narrowed. "That was it."

He felt his cheeks grow warm. "I'm sorry."

"I'm flattered, really."

"You look great." She did. The woman he'd represented had looked like a shell of a person by that point in her marriage. This woman looked alive and vibrant.

"It's amazing what ditching a husband can do for a person's metabolism and self-esteem. And I have you to thank." This time, when her eyes narrowed, they had a purpose. He recognized the attraction, and he took an automatic step backward.

"How long have you worked for O'Keeley's?"

She lifted a shoulder. "A couple weeks by now. I knew you were an owner. I saw you a few other times but never had a chance to say anything."

"Well," he began, taking another step away and toward the safety of his office. Kami leaned on the counter, straight out inviting with her eyes. They were gorgeous eyes. "I have a pile of paperwork to start on."

"Maybe we can talk some other time? You know, after work?"

Might as well lay it on the line. He stopped in his retreat and smiled at her. "I'd like that, Kami Dawson, but seeing as I'm your employer, I'm afraid our conversations need to be limited to work and work hours." He shrugged. "My brother's rules." And his. He never wanted a long-term relationship and working alongside someone he found interesting one night, didn't bode well for anyone.

The disappointment was evident, but she didn't argue. She simply nodded and turned back to the register. His eyes landed on Katie, watching the interaction, although she would be too far away to hear anything.

Katie shook her head. At one point, Katie had issued similar invitations to him and had been turned away. It was a small joke between his family and her now, both happy as friends. Cathal winked, and Katie fanned herself before laughing.

He walked into the silence of Brogan's office and closed the door. He'd have to let his brother know about Kami. At least, with everyone aware, they'd know Cathal wasn't trying to pull anything. He tossed his keys and phone into the desk drawer and powered on the computer. A stack of unopened mail sat in the middle of the desk with a note on top.

To give you something to do- S

Selena. His sister-in-law was so thoughtful. He snorted and tossed the note in the trashcan. Brogan had found his female counterpart. She lightened his brother up from being a straitlaced ass most of the time, but they both loved running the business. The paperwork they could keep. Cathal enjoyed interacting with the people.

He opened the top letter. It came from an attorney's office he was knowledgeable of. One that didn't always play above board. All attorneys pursued every avenue possible to gain a favorable outcome for their client, but, at least for him, he'd never go against his ethics to do so.

Cathal scanned the letter, standing up as he read the meat of it. They were being sued.

He took the letter and left the restaurant. Brogan might have declared Sunday his day off, but Rian never did. Since the man lived within walking distance, he'd pay him a personal visit to deliver the good news.

"MOTHER—"

Fiona pinched the bridge of her nose and waited while her mother cried. Long, drawn-out sobs that would look as fake as they sounded. To her mom, they weren't fake. She honestly thought she was that upset. But in a snap, she'd be over the issue and moving on with life.

"I just don't know why you're doing this to us." Her mom paused and blew her nose. "It's been almost a year. When are you coming back?"

"Mom, I'm only thirty minutes away." Her parents lived a

little north of Atlanta, not on the other side of the country. But no one, not her friends, not her parents, ever came to visit. Hell, her friends hadn't even tried to contact her since the incident.

"I meant back to the family. Your father just hasn't been the same since you left. He and Hugo have worked hard in the business. They could use your help." She sniffed. "You and Hugo should try again."

For the business. Her dad wanted her there so he could hand over the company to his son-in-law that he'd groomed to take over.

"You were there, Mom. He was naked on the bed with Wren." Her description of the situation went from polite to a little vulgar to try and get her mom to admit what she'd seen. But her mom's mental stability was always a little frail, and Fiona's dad easily influenced her.

"Fiona, I told you I wasn't sure what I saw."

"You picked up Wren's underwear, Mom!"

"Maybe," she mumbled. "Yes. I agree, but Hugo says that wasn't him."

Fiona tossed her hand in the air as she paced her apartment. Granted, Hugo had bolted into the bathroom that connected with another guest suite, leaving Wren to fumble for an explanation alone. But Hugo's butt had a very distinct birthmark on it. One that reminded her of a Dalmatian's spot. And Wren even admitted it at first before changing her story.

Both of them were drunk.

Still, not an excuse.

"I'm not going back over this. I know what I saw. If you want to play Dad's little game to get me to come back home, that's fine, but I'm not going to budge. I like my life now. I like running a bar." She wanted to make it successful.

"But you have a degree in economics. You and Hugo are going to take over the operations once you get married."

Still in the future tense. Her mom never gave up. Fiona didn't want to run an international shipping company. Yes, it was profitable, but some things were more important to her.

Pride was one of them. Sanity was another. She couldn't exist around people who questioned her if she didn't go along with their version of reality.

"I'm done talking about this. I'd still like to see you next weekend."

"Oh, I don't know. Your father, dear, would be mad. He thinks that if I stay away, that you'll come back home."

Fiona bit her lip against the frustration. The issue wasn't her dad wanting her back home, it was her dad wanting Hugo in the family. He'd taught him the ropes, pegged him to take over his "empire" and Fiona had ruined that. Actually, Hugo destroyed that when he decided to play CEO and secretary with Wren.

"Let me know later this week, then. I love you."

"Love you, too," her mom replied, sounding as though nothing had upset her to begin with.

Fiona picked up her keys and purse and jogged out the door. Sunday was her only day off, and she took advantage of every second. Her yoga class started in fifteen minutes. The April weather hovered in the mid-seventies, and the new leaves were bright green. She loved spring. Everything was born again. That's how she wanted her life to feel. Fresh. New. Instead, her parents and ex were a constant reminder that she could never really move forward. Not until that situation was resolved.

She kept her head down, her thoughts running over and over Hugo, replaying the scene in her mind.

Two feet appeared in her vision.

She snapped her head up, coming face-to-face with Cathal. He held a piece of paper in his hand, and for a quick second, the cocky look he wore was absent.

It changed his face. The man was attractive when he was all smiles, cracking jokes and making everyone around him laugh. Right then, with a small worry line in between his brows and his eyes pinched tight with stress, he looked angry and sexy-as-hell.

He blinked. "Fiona?"

Her breath hitched, and her face grew warm with the way he said her name.

But he ruined it a second later. That damn, silly grin appeared as he tilted his head to the side. "What is the most beautiful woman in Atlanta doing out this time of day?"

"I'm headed to yoga." She motioned at his suit. "I didn't realize you wore a suit every day of the week."

"It's Brogan's rule. I'm actually supposed to be at the restaurant but needed to run an errand." He shifted closer, his blue eyes matching the sky behind him. "I'm glad I ran into you."

She moved to the side, away from his incredible maleness. The smell of his cologne or aftershave was more pronounced when not in her bar. More lethal to her senses.

"I figured you'd still be curled up around some lucky woman from last night." Her tone of voice reminded her of a bitter shrew. She hated it. That wasn't who she was. Not deep down. Hugo had done that to her.

His smile didn't falter. "Ah, Fiona, it doesn't take luck for that to happen. Not for you."

She rolled her eyes. Playboy. "I need to go. Have a good day."

"I will now that I've seen you." He winked when she glanced back up.

She shook her head and walked away, hating that she was as susceptible to his charm as every other female. She'd already fallen in love with another smooth-talking man and look where that had gotten her: humiliation. Even though she knew the fault lie with Hugo and Wren, a small part of her ego wondered why she hadn't been enough for him.

What was she missing?

Nothing. She straightened her shoulders and pushed open the door to the yoga studio with a bright smile on her face. She wanted this life, not the life she'd set herself up for with Hugo. Big house. Great career. No love. There had been love there, once, a long time ago. Back in college, she'd made big plans with him. But at some point, she'd fallen out of love.

Unfortunately, she never broke off the relationship, and it turned out that Hugo didn't really love her either. Maybe, if she did have feelings for Hugo, she'd have fought harder instead of walking away from that life and her wedding day.

3

"We'll figure this out." Selena paced back and forth in front of a small box fan in the office at O'Keeley's. With her bare feet swollen and her blue tank top stretched tight over her stomach, she looked like a cute blueberry. Not that Cathal would point that out to his pregnant sister-in-law. They had the air conditioning set on sixty-seven, the coldest Brogan said he'd run it without offering free sweatshirts to their patrons.

Poor Selena was still hot.

"Someone is actually suing us for over-serving them at the bar?" Rian sipped on a glass of wine, one ankle crossed over his knee while Mara, his girlfriend, sat beside him on the low, leather sofa. "Is that a thing?"

"Yes." Cathal stood, facing the group, surprisingly sober. He'd helped them before with legal troubles, but nothing of this magnitude. His skills would be put to the test with the lawsuit. He'd spent the past week on the phone with the other law firm, getting the details. "It's rather serious. Someone left our restaurant and hit a pedestrian.

Thankfully, the man he hit survived, but he's suing the drunk driver and us."

"I don't see how this happened. No one gets drunk here. For all we know, the man made two other stops before getting in his car. If we're liable, then we'll settle. But I'm not going to let someone take advantage of us just because the guy came here to eat dinner. We'll fight it if that's the case." Selena's face flushed red from either the conversation or from the baby. "We've got you to defend us."

Cathal held up his hands. "True. You know I'll be the first one to say we're not at fault, but it's not that easy. It's illegal to serve alcohol to a visibly intoxicated person."

"So, we have to prove we didn't do this." Brogan leaned against the wall, his eyes trained on his wife. With less than a month to go for Selena's delivery, he'd been hovering around her, like he was ready to catch the baby should it make a surprise appearance. Knowing Brogan, he'd already read every book on the subject and participated in a midwifery class. The damn man was probably certified.

"Basically. We have cameras. Those will need to be reviewed. And we may still be on the hook for some settlement. If this goes to a trial, the jury is not going to be very friendly toward us. All sympathy will go toward the man injured. Especially in the south. There's still a very conservative approach to drinking." Cathal just hoped he had enough skill to mount a good defense. He'd reach out to his colleagues if he needed it. Their restaurant had come too far to be blown away by this.

"For the time being, let's give our bartenders extra training. Document it. I don't want this to happen again." Brogan loosened his tie. "Selena, if you're up to it—"

She snapped her head around.

He held up his hands. "I know. Just because you're

pregnant doesn't mean you can't work. You've gone over that before. If you can, give the waitstaff a course. Cathal, I'll leave the bartenders to you."

Cathal frowned. "Why?"

"Because you spend your time with more bartenders than the rest of us."

He didn't like that reason, but he couldn't deny it. "While I have you all gathered, I'd like to make mention of a past relationship with our newest bartender, Kami Dawson."

"Shit," Rian mumbled.

Brogan ran a hand over his face.

Selena and Mara shared a look, both smiling. Mara patted Rian's knee. "Rian's just jealous he can't play the field like you anymore."

"No. I'm more embarrassed that he's played the field so much it's starting to become a measurable amount in a city this size. What exactly do you think the percentage is, little brother?"

Cathal held his hand up, not the least bit offended. "It's not measurable, seeing as I don't keep a tally."

Both the women giggled while his brothers rolled their eyes.

"I represented Kami in her divorce settlement."

"And you didn't hit on her?" Rian asked. "Not to say this in front of Mara, but I've seen Kami. She's your type."

Selena perked up. "Type? You like exotic looking females? I didn't know that."

Brogan tried to cover his laugh but failed. "No, darling. His type is female."

"Basically." Cathal set his hands on his hips and stared down his family. All of them. "And I've never been involved with a client. Ever. Not before or after. Just like I'll never get involved with an employee." He hitched his thumb at Brogan. "I have a little more restraint than him."

They all laughed, well, except for Brogan. He glared. Serves the man right. Cathal would never deny that Selena was perfect for him, but Brogan still hated to admit that breaking his own strict rules was the only way he'd found her.

"But I will say if I'm reading Kami's signals right, she's interested. I just want to put it out there. If you hear anything, don't believe it before you ask." Cathal rubbed his hands together. "Now, it's ten o'clock on a Friday, would anyone like to join me at a certain bar?"

"Just like that? You aren't worried about the lawsuit?" asked Mara.

"I am. Definitely. I've worked on it all week." And he'd continue to work toward an answer until he found one. "That's all the more reason to find a distraction." He shifted his weight, flicking his focus between his brothers. "I started a new case today. Mediating a divorce." And based on the wife's testimony, which he believed, the jackass soon-to-be ex-husband had laid his hands on her. Left bruises. And possibly struck her son, although she'd been crying while explaining the situation, so Cathal needed a little more time to understand what'd happened.

Both the brothers straightened. "You alright?" Brogan asked.

"I can come out with you if you need me to." Rian added.

"I'll be fine." He slept like shit, more than usual, whenever he worked a case like that, but nothing was new. "I'm not looking forward to having to meet the husband." He huffed and took a step toward the door. "I might not get my hands on him, but I can get my hands on his money. He owes her at least half his earnings and then some if I have anything to say about it."

He left O'Keeley's and climbed into his Mercedes, tossing his suit jacket in the passenger seat and loosening his tie. He never dressed down to go to Fiona's, always coming from his law firm or O'Keeley's. The drive to his apartment was quick. He'd walk there, leaving himself open to drink however much he wanted. Probably not at Fiona's, though. He never drank to excess there. He didn't want her to see him as a drunk.

He parked and walked down the road, rolling the sleeves on his buttoned-down shirt. Rian had joked with him once that Cathal had a small crush on Fiona.

Small didn't begin to describe it.

The security guard, Chuck, stood from his stool when Cathal approached. "Don't cause any trouble tonight."

"I never plan on it."

"I'll kick you out."

"Fiona kicks me out herself." He patted the big man as he walked by. "So, don't worry yourself over it." He let the loud music and eclectic atmosphere soothe away the stress from the pending lawsuit against O'Keeley's.

He liked Fiona's bar. He assumed it fit her personality. Getting to know her better would happen. Someday.

Seeing Fiona, her red hair piled on top of her head, her purple tank top a little lower than usual, lightened his mood considerably. Until he spotted the sot down the bar staring. Not just the typical male glance of appreciation. No. It surprised him the man's tongue wasn't hanging out of his mouth and dragging the ground.

His regular spot at the end of her bar would remain empty.

Cathal squeezed past several guests trying to get Fiona's

attention for a drink and sat down on an empty stool beside the man with the roaming eyes. Hell, the guy didn't even try to conceal every lusty thought that floated through his mind.

Fiona slowed down as she passed by, glanced toward the end corner of her bar, and then back at Cathal. She set a paper napkin on the bar in front of him.

"What are you up to?"

The man beside Cathal leaned forward a little. "Hey," he said, his eyes barely making it off her cleavage.

Cathal hitched a thumb toward the wandering eyes next to him. "You have a fan."

"And that bothers you?"

"Of course." He grinned and ignored the exasperation in her expression. "Everyone knows you have a crush on me, Fiona."

The man looked at Cathal with a shocked expression. "You? No. She winked at me earlier. I'm just waiting until her shift is over, then I'm taking her home."

Fiona set her hand on her hip. "I don't think I invited you to my house."

Cathal opened his mouth, but she held her finger up at him without a glance his direction. "You either."

Cathal chuckled. "Worth a shot."

The man beside him shook his head. "Nope. I don't give up that easily."

"You might as well give up, honey, it's not going to happen. Today. Tomorrow. Next week." Fiona turned and grabbed the whiskey off the shelf. "Here." She passed Cathal a glass of the amber liquid. "I don't need a babysitter if you want to move to your usual spot."

The man reached out and held onto Fiona's wrist as she started to pull away.

The whiskey in the glass sloshed over the edge as Cathal let it drop to the bar. He clamped his hand on top of the man's wrist, squeezing. Not hard enough to break anything. Yet.

"I suggest you let her go," Cathal murmured in a low voice. He'd shifted his back to Fiona slightly, blocking the man's view of her. He felt her tug her arm. The man still didn't release her. Mistake.

"I'm not playing with you." Cathal squeezed his hand tighter.

The man's lips pressed into a tight, thin line, trying to ignore the pain. Cathal squeezed harder.

His eyes widened. He let go of Fiona.

Cathal, his hand still wrapped around the man's wrist, pushed the guy away from the bar, took a step with him, but didn't release him. Tugging him back, the man stumbled forward like a rag doll.

He stopped right in front of Cathal, swaying slightly. Cathal didn't bother to conceal the fury he felt in his veins. The man must have seen it since the fight and color drained from his face.

"If you lay a hand on her again, I will make sure you leave with something broken."

The man held his free hand up. "You're crazy."

Cathal smiled, without warmth, probably looking a little deranged. "Yes." He released him with a shove.

The man tripped a few times but left the bar, pushing past the bouncer who walked his way. Too late.

Fiona said something to the bouncer. The big man looked at Cathal one more time before going back to his post at the door.

She sat a new whiskey glass down at his usual seat and remained, waiting on him. He liked the feeling, her wanting him there, inviting him to sit down, even if she didn't say the words.

"Thank you," she mumbled, drying off a glass that she pulled out of the washer. "I wasn't expecting him to do that. What made you go sit over there?"

Cathal took a sip of his whiskey, his eyes locked with hers, until he flicked them down to her cleavage above her tank top and back up. "He liked the view, and I didn't like his enjoyment of it."

Fiona looked down, tugging up on her top. "I didn't realize it was so low until I started moving around the bar tonight." She held her arms out. "But seeing that I have no employees to provide me a moment to run and change, I'm stuck."

Cathal rose and ducked underneath the back of the counter.

She backed up a step.

Was she scared of him? He didn't like the thought. "I'm going to help. Run home and change."

"But..."

"But? I run the bar at O'Keeley's. Surely you trust me by now?"

"Yes." She pouted, looking down at her hands. "I'm just not used to relying on anyone lately."

He set a hand on her shoulder, trying to avoid the lure of her cleavage. He was no better than the sleazy guy. Instead, he focused on the smoothness of her skin under his fingers. Immediately, he knew it'd been wrong to touch her.

He'd want to do it again.

His thumb brushed along the edge of her neck.

She didn't jerk away, which surprised him. "Run home. I'm fine." He pointed to the tiny camera on the ceiling. "You can review the tape to make sure I don't walk out of here with cash if you want to."

"No." She moved away, snagging her purse from underneath the counter. "I will go change." She pulled up her tank top again. "Because it is bothering me. He wasn't the first drunk guy to take notice tonight."

Cathal bet not. He waited for her to leave the bar before turning back toward the crowd.

It was different than serving at O'Keeley's. On Friday or Saturday night, a crowd of people piled around the bar at O'Keeley's, but it wasn't set up to be a bar for gathering. More like waiting on tables or a few drinks after work. Nothing like the crush of people around Fiona's bar.

He started at one end and made his way down and then back again, taking orders, filling drinks, and making change. He enjoyed the work in general. He ignored the four phone numbers slipped his way. Three women and a man. He was flattered, to be sure, but none of them were Fiona.

It was a surprise that he'd rather be there, helping her, than curled up next to someone else.

Hell, he'd rather be curled up next to Fiona.

A hand brushed his arm. "I'm back." She scanned the crowd. "Of all the nights, it's busier than usual. I'm sorry but thank you."

She'd returned in a white shirt, plain, the corner tucked into the front of her jeans. Her face was devoid of most makeup it seemed. She looked fresh and young.

She held up her hand. "Don't look at me that way." She moved a step away.

"What way?"

She twisted her lips to the side. "Like you were going to kiss me."

"I wanted to kiss you, so I guess my look was correct."

"You're horrible."

Cathal shifted closer to her. "That's a good thing, right?"

She laughed. He enjoyed making her laugh. "I'll get this under control; you can go back to your drink." She pointed at the end of the bar. "On the house tonight."

"No need."

"You worked for nearly forty-five minutes for me. I think I can spare you a glass of whiskey."

He took an order and another. He'd stay back there until closing if it'd help her. They worked side-by-side, the crush of the crowd not giving them much time to socialize. But he'd managed to find ways to touch her like brushing his arm against her shoulder. Each time he reached around her for a bottle, he was rewarded with an exasperated huff that made him smile.

A little after midnight, the pace finally slowed.

"Thank you, again," Fiona said, leaning against the wall behind the bar as she sipped a glass of water. "Are you sure you won't let me pay you?"

"Yes. I am. I'd either be sitting at your bar or home."

"Or drinking at another bar."

He ran a finger over his mouth. "Ah, probably." He shrugged, feeling a little out of sorts. This wasn't familiar territory to him. He dropped back to what he was good at.

With a slow smile, he paused a moment. "I'd rather be here with you."

She sighed. "And we're back to that." She set her water down and gave him a gentle shove toward the door. "Go on. The crowd has died down. I can handle the rest."

He let her push him. Why did flirting seem to work with, literally, every other female he encountered, but it didn't work for Fiona?

Cathal pulled up at the edge of the bar, a second before

he ducked underneath. He turned quickly, Fiona stumbling against his chest at the sudden stop. And he forgot what he was going to say.

A faint trace of honeysuckles enveloped him. That was her scent. It suited her. They'd had a massive honeysuckle bush in their backyard in Ireland. Wild. It grew along the stone wall at the edge of their property.

She pushed away, leaving his arms empty and taking away the memory. "Sorry."

"Please, never apologize for touching me." This time, when he grinned, he didn't contain the wicked edge to it.

She took another step back.

"Fiona, pull out your phone. I'm going to do something I've not done in years."

She frowned. "What do you need it for?"

"I'm going to give a woman my phone number."

She sat a hand on her hip. "Are you serious?"

"Yes. If it's you calling me, I'll be happy to answer."

"Why?"

"Because, the way I see it, you might need me at some point. If that happens, I want to make sure you have it." He rattled off the number, forcing her to pull out her phone. She read it back off to him like she'd taken someone's order. Clinical and cute.

"Great." She slipped her phone into her back pocket. "Just don't expect me to call you for a date."

A small part of him did hope she'd reach out to him, but having it confirmed didn't hurt his feelings. Fiona needed a man to pursue her. And, yes, he was that man.

But at the rate they were moving, it'd be next Christmas before she'd give him the green light to make a move.

"I want you to call me the next time your bar is slammed that way." At her expected eye roll, something she seemed to do often with him, he stepped forward, lightly gripping her upper arms. God, he wanted to lean down and find the source of that delicious scent, but he remained upright. "I'm serious. I'll be happy to leave wherever I'm posted up to come and help you. I had fun tonight."

"Don't you normally help at O'Keeley's?" Did she shift toward him? "I don't want to take you away from your job."

"Other than events, they survive just fine without me. In fact, we have pretty shitty bartenders over there. If we have an event, I may offer to hire you." His hands glided up her arms to rest at the curve of her neck, his fingers threading into the hair.

She blinked and moved away. "Yeah, well, I'll keep that in mind." She wiggled her phone in the air. "You know, about calling if I get in a bind again." She looked at her phone, serious. "I wonder how much I could make auctioning off your telephone number to the women in Atlanta."

He smirked even though his body begged for her to come back into his arms. "Not very much, I'm afraid." He ducked under the bar, needing to leave before he really made a pass at her.

For some strange reason, he *wanted* her to be the one to make a move. Because his Fiona didn't fall into a man's arms when he promised her a night of fun; Fiona needed more than a warm body.

Cathal wasn't sure what the hell she needed. Or if he could even give it to her.

4

The phone rang a third time. Fiona darted across her apartment to grab it before whoever called hung up. The caller id made her groan. Hugo. Her ex-fiancé. She answered, hating that it turned her stomach into knots.

"Hey, what do you need?" It wasn't a polite answer. But Hugo wasn't a polite man. He'd proved that when he slept with her maid-of-honor.

He chuckled in a forced, high-society way. Patronizing. "Ah, Fiona, still the same spunk."

Spunk? He was blind. She wasn't spunky. She was mad.

"Yeah. Sure. Tell me what you wanted or I'm hanging up." Because she didn't want to talk to him. He made her skin feel as though a thousand spiders ran across it.

"Just calling to check-in. See how you're doing. See if you need anything."

"If I need anything, I'll get it myself."

He chuckled again. The sound grated on Fiona's nerves. "I'm sure you will. You are a competent woman. I miss you. I want us to set a date for this whole debacle to end."

"If by debacle you mean me having a job and a life

outside of yours, then don't hold your breath. I'm staying here. I own a bar. I'm not coming back to you."

A massive sigh broke the silence. "Oh, Fiona, when will you understand that life goes on beyond the tantrum you've thrown. We have a major business to run. Your father, all the employees, they're counting on us."

"Goodbye, Hugo." She hung up because calling him a self-centered, imbecile, with the I.Q. of a donkey, would bring her down to the level where "tantrum" was a good description.

The phone cleared, and belatedly she realized that she'd pulled up Cathal's number. She wouldn't call him, but the fact he'd given it to her was a surprise, especially after he admitted to never handing it out to any other woman. She supposed that was a smart choice on his part. Nothing like dozens and dozens of women begging for dates.

She snorted and shook her head. He'd been determined to sit at the end of *her* bar and harass *her* every night. But last week, he'd been different. For a brief moment, maybe two minutes, he'd not had that goofy, flirty grin stretched across his lips. And when he'd touched her, she'd barely contained the shiver that raced across her skin. His eyes narrowed, just a touch at the corners like he was trying to figure himself out as well as her reaction.

Even though that side of Cathal had intrigued her, she'd stick to the shallow end of the pool when it came to the youngest O'Keeley. Probably better if she only dipped her feet in the baby pool.

But tonight, was Saturday night. If he missed Friday night, he always strolled into her bar on Saturday. And she'd be there, ready for his charm. His jokes. His smile. Because even though his playboy attitude didn't appeal to her, Cathal, the man with the blue eyes and pale golden skin, still sped up her heartbeat. And, like today, he seemed to pop into her thoughts more and more.

She shook her head, trying to get rid of the sinking feeling that she was no better than those other women looking for a one-night stand with him. Because she didn't want the one night. She didn't want two nights. She wanted to stay away from Cathal before she ended up in the same position.

Hugo was a playboy.

Cathal was a playboy.

Both charmed women blind. In the case of Hugo, he'd even charmed Fiona's dad and all her friends, blind.

She grabbed her keys and left the apartment. Going into the bar gave her something else to do besides sit there and think of her ex-fiancé. Because doing that would piss her off all over again. People came into her bar to buy a drink and sit with their troubles. No one went to a bar to watch a surly bartender slam drinks on the counter.

Fiona walked the couple blocks to her bar. After unlocking the door, she picked up the mail from the floor where it'd been delivered.

Again, an envelope from the department that authorized her liquor license was included. She didn't know who kept trying to get her license revoked, but ever since the first time, she'd been on top of things. This time, it was a threat of over-serving individuals due to a pattern of aggressive or violent behavior at her bar.

Again. It always happened after Cathal got into a fight.

But he'd never been drunk.

She headed to her office to type up a reply to the letter. After the first notice, she'd gone down to the office in person. It seemed as though a room of secretaries and clerks ran it. Finding anyone with authority was impossible.

Pulling out her phone, she almost dialed Cathal's number. If she saw him tonight, she'd ask him about O'Keeley's. Was this a common issue? Did everyone get 'threats' of their license being suspended?

She didn't want her bar to fail. It'd been open for almost a year. A year on her own. And it'd confirmed that she was entirely over Hugo and almost glad Wren had ruined everything.

LAST NIGHT HAD ENDED up being an exciting night. Although he'd missed his set date with Fiona at her bar, the band O'Keeley's hired to play Saturday night had ended up having a fiddle player with them.

And Cathal had joined in the fun.

It was after one-thirty by the time they closed, officially putting him at closing time for Fiona. Going to her place to help her close had crossed his mind. The four glasses of whiskey begged him for another shot with his redhead. But the small amount of a decent, sober fellow avoided the situation.

He wouldn't screw up how far they'd come.

Fiona liked him. Even if as a friend, she'd liked him enough to trust him with her bar while she went to change clothes. It'd been a shame she had to change out of that purple tank top. Fiona definitely had the perfect set of curves that a man dreamed about, even on a Sunday.

Mara opened the door to the restaurant. She waved to a few of their staff before heading in his direction. She was a beautiful woman. Her ebony skin offset against a white blouse. Her hair swept back away from her face. And she was too good for the likes of his brother.

He finished straightening the chair at a table and smiled in her direction. "Good morning, Mara. I hate to say this, seeing as you might leave me, but Rian's not here."

"I know. I left him in the condo, yelling at food. He's trying some new recipe, and I can't take it any longer. I keep thinking he wants the food to argue back with him or something." She held her hands out. "So, put me to work."

Cathal loved that about Mara. She'd stepped into the family and completed one more missing piece he didn't realize they missed. But two women would be enough. Cathal could never marry.

Not that he was against marriage. In an ideal world, where the past wouldn't be a constant reminder of how much damage he was capable of, he'd find a sweet girl and settle down. But he'd never find a woman he cared for that much and put her in the position of marrying a man who'd murdered someone.

"Waitress, it is..." His words drifted off.

Fiona stood in the doorway with a man. A man whose hand pressed along her lower back as the hostess took them to a seat.

Mara glanced over her shoulder. "That's the bartender from that bar where Rian first kissed me. I don't remember her name-"

"Fiona."

"Ah, you know her?" Mara smiled and nudged him. "How well do you know her?"

Not well enough in his book. And now, on a Sunday, she was here with another man. A date? Cathal took a step, but Mara stopped him with a light touch on his arm.

"Whoa there, cowboy, you don't look like you're in a mood to talk to customers."

"I'm in a fine mood," he gritted out between his teeth.

Mara raised her eyebrows. "You obviously don't like seeing her with another man. Let me wait on their table." She patted him on his chest. "I'll get the dirt on him for you."

"Dirt?" He tore his gaze away from the man holding out Fiona's chair and shifted his focus to Mara. "What do you mean dirt?"

"I'll make small talk. It'll be easy enough. She should remember me after Rian's epic kiss in her bar. Then I'll introduce myself to the guy."

"How is that dirt?" Cathal didn't want to play the game. He wanted the girl. He didn't give two shits about the guy.

"How she introduces him says a lot. Just give me a chance. You busting up their date like the Hulk won't help."

"You're the second person to compare me to the Hulk."

Mara winked. "I've heard the stories." She handed him her purse. "Will you put this in the office? I'll go take their order now."

He stood there a moment longer, holding onto Mara's purse and staring at Fiona.

Fiona turned and spotted him. She half smiled and lifted a hand.

He started to lift his hand but realized he still held Mara's big brown purse. He turned and stalked to the office to lock it up for her. Dumb. He was a straight idiot when it came to Fiona, and he didn't know why. Women were easy for him. Talking to them. Flirting with them. But not with Fiona.

Cathal came out as Mara walked to the bar. She drummed her hands on the bar top. Their bartender, Kami, was gone for some reason, so Cathal ducked underneath the edge.

"I have an order and some dirt." Mara leaned on the

counter and held up her pad. "Fiona would like a mimosa, and Derek—"

"Derek?"

"Yes, Derek, would like a Bloody Mary. But no celery." Mara tapped her hand on the bar. "He'd also not like those deranged looks you keep sending him."

Cathal started making their drinks, ignoring Mara's comment. Deranged? He'd admit to jealousy when it came to Fiona. Derek wasn't above Cathal feeling jealous over the jammy bastard.

"I'll take these."

Mara frowned. "Do you think that's the best idea?"

"I always have great ideas, and this is one of them."

"But you left the Hulk in the office, right?"

Cathal winked at her. "You can't separate Bruce Banner from the Hulk, but he's tightly tucked away for the moment," a good reminder as to why he could never have a long-term, serious relationship with Fiona. But he'd already established he was selfish and wanted a little bit of time with his redhead before he moved on.

He took the drinks up to Fiona and Derek. The man didn't even have the decency to tuck in his shirt on a date. "Here are your drinks." He sat them down, ignoring Fiona's sharp look.

He watched Derek as he held out his hand. "Hi, I'm Cathal O'Keeley, part-owner of the restaurant."

The man smirked. "Oh, yeah?" He shook with a clammy, wimpy hand. "Nice place you've got here."

"Thanks." Cathal turned to Fiona. Her eyes were wary. Probably for a good reason. "Hi."

"Hey."

Derek motioned between them as he took a sip of his drink. "Do you two know each other?"

"Yes." Cathal left it at that.

Fiona sighed like speaking was a chore. "He's a...friend of mine."

"Yes. Friends. *Best* friends, if I'd have to qualify us." He left. He didn't need to see any more of Derek to know he wasn't for Fiona.

Cathal walked back to the bar, spotting Kami again at her position now. "How's Selena doing?" Kami asked, leaning on the counter, her cleavage on display and looking like she'd tempt most other men. Not him.

"Fine. Ready for the babe to arrive, I know that."

"Let me know if you want me to pick up more shifts. I can work anytime you want me to." She smiled in a slow seductive way that didn't do a thing for him.

He nodded and moved along, not stopping until he was safely in his office. Certain women, women like Kami, who were told the rules and still pushed it, bothered him. He'd have to mention it to Brogan, again. He'd never want someone to lose their job, but he wouldn't risk the business for Kami's incessant flirting.

Cathal reached for an envelope atop the pile of mail that Selena had for him to go through. He appreciated feeling part of the business, but nearly half of the correspondence he opened, he set to the side for her or Brogan to figure out what to do with it. He knew they had a system that worked.

After sorting the mail, he focused on the lawsuit and the research he'd printed to go over.

Fiona knocked on the door to the office. She stood just inside, leaning against the opening. "Hi."

He rose from behind the desk. She'd sought him out. "Hi."

"I'm about to head out."

Cathal glanced at his watch. He'd been working for nearly an hour. "Did you enjoy your lunch?"

"The food was delicious." She glanced over her shoulder. "The fact my date is hitting on your bartender pretty much sums up the dating aspect."

Cathal smiled.

She sneered, the expression cute. "Don't look so damn pleased."

"I'm not. I hate it that the man didn't obviously make you the center of his world, which is where you should be."

Fiona rolled her eyes like she usually did, but a small flush on her cheeks caught his attention. Had his comment caused that?

"I'm sorry I missed this weekend," he said.

She hesitated. Was having a normal conversation with him that hard for her? "Why did you?"

"Because I was working here. It may be like that for a while, hit or miss, with the babe on the way. I'm trying to give them more time at home together. Brogan's worried about Selena."

She held his gaze before looking away. "That's nice of you."

"You sound surprised."

"No. I'm not. Really." She ran a hand through her hair, looking unsure of herself. "Then, I guess I'll see you later. Let me go pry Derek away from your bartender."

"Her name is Kami, and he's welcome to her at this point."

Fiona crossed her arms. "I saw her leaned over the counter, issuing you an invitation. At least, that's how it looked from my vantage point."

"It doesn't matter how many times I remind her of the rules. She doesn't care."

"And what rules are those?"

Cathal rolled his shoulders, hating the distance between him and Fiona, but he'd stay put for the time being. Fiona needed to understand that he was a regular guy and not whatever she saw in him.

"No dating our employees. Aside from Selena with Brogan, that is. That wasn't supposed to happen, but nothing can stop true love and fate."

"Do you believe in true love?"

He stepped around the desk, slipped his hands into his suit pants pockets, and walked toward her. She didn't back away but watched him with an open appraisal he was glad to finally see.

"I suppose I do. Ireland does have some of the most romantic poets in history. And it's hard to deny when Rian found his Mara. Brogan found Selena."

She tilted her head to the side. "What about you?"

"Me? No."

Her sarcastic laugh made him pause. "Because that would require monogamy, right?"

Ah. So, was that Fiona's hesitancy with him? He sighed. "No. Monogamy doesn't worry me." He lowered his head, watching her with as much intensity as he felt inside.

Her lips parted with a sharp intake of breath.

"If I found one woman to be with, and one woman alone, I wouldn't have any trouble remaining faithful to her. The difference is I don't *want* to find that one woman."

"Do you want to be alone forever?" she asked with soft disbelief in her voice. Maybe it did sound crazy, but it was the only way he could live his life.

"Alone?" He held his arms out and motioned around him. "I'm surrounded by family. By customers. By friends. I'm not alone."

She stepped back from the door, her eyes still watching him, reading him in a way that made him uncomfortable. She could try and analyze him all she wanted. No woman deserved him as a husband.

"I have a hard time thinking that will be enough for you. I'll see you later," she said with her serious expression making her forehead crease into cute little lines.

"I'm looking forward to it." He smiled until she left the doorway. That was as close as he'd get to discussing his ideas on relationships with Fiona. He liked her right where she was, just outside those deeper emotions he chose to ignore.

But she'd made him start to think about the past and his future. Both scary places for him to travel.

He turned back to the pile of shit on the desk and the lawsuit he'd pulled out to address. The lawyers and judge needed a formal reply. They'd fight it, obviously. If the man left O'Keeley's intoxicated, they'd take responsibility. How much was their responsibility versus the man driving the car was part of the question. They'd finally made a profit after dumping out every penny they had to buy the building they currently occupied. They wouldn't stumble back into debt unnecessarily.

5

Fiona walked into the towering, concrete building in the middle of downtown Atlanta that housed the department for the liquor licenses. Her footsteps echoed on the marble floors. She'd finally scored an appointment and hoped to get her questions answered. Like how they seemed to have a spy in her bar since she got these notices almost every damn time something happened.

No one she knew worked for this division of the city. The first thoughts were that one of Hugo's friends, her ex-friends, might be pulling a few strings on his behalf, but no one came to mind.

She approached the man at a receptionist's desk, giving off as much confidence as she could muster. "I'm here to see Mickey DeLaurey." She wasn't sure if that was a man or a woman. "I have an appointment."

"Right. If you can, please take a seat." He pointed at a long line of plastic chairs, one step up from the kind she'd seen around backyard pools. And filled with others waiting. "She'll come to get you when she's ready."

Fiona glanced at her watch. Her bar opened at three on Mondays. It was one-thirty now. This was when she regretted not hiring at least part-time help. But she needed every dollar she could spare. Her parents paid for her apartment and her car. She would have gladly moved somewhere less expensive, but her mother insisted she stay in an exclusive condominium complex. A security guard on duty, twenty-four seven. Tall iron fences to keep anyone nefarious out. Fiona knew it hadn't anything to do with her living alone in Atlanta and everything with keeping up appearances.

As much as she wanted to throw her parents' money back in their face, accepting it had given her the freedom to build up her business. She reinvested her profits. Her degree didn't help her learn to make the perfect Manhattan, but she knew how to run a business.

Fiona bounced her leg crossed knee and looked at her watch again. Two-fifteen.

Two-thirty.

It was getting close. The meeting could last five minutes or an hour. No way to tell. She sucked in a breath through her nose, knowing there was only one person she could call for help. Calling Cathal for a massive favor beat out giving up her appointment and risking them shutting her down. That really would be the end of her bar. The constant beat of pride that she'd clung to pounded in her body as she pulled out her cell phone.

Pressing his name, she closed her eyes and grimaced when he answered. She'd done it. She'd called the man.

"Cathal?"

After a beat of silence, he chuckled. "Fiona?"

"I need a huge favor from you."

"Now?" He mumbled something, obviously to whoever

was in the room with him. He was probably at O'Keeley's. "What is it?"

"I received a letter, again, threatening to suspend my liquor license."

He spoke again to someone else before the background noise disappeared. "Alright. Do you want me to look at it?"

"No. I understand it well enough. I'm in the department now. Finally, I got an appointment with them. The problem is that my bar is supposed to open in-" she glanced at her watch "-shit. Fifteen minutes and they haven't called me back yet." She raised her voice, aiming a nasty look toward the receptionist. "And I *had* an appointment for *one- thirty*." The man behind the desk remained unaffected by her outburst.

"Do you want me to take over the meeting with the liquor license department or go open your bar?"

She slouched back in her chair. She hadn't figured he offer to come down and relieve her. But at this point, it felt personal, the constant threats to close her bar and ruin her dream.

"Can you open the bar? I keep getting these notices, and I'd like to get to the bottom of it."

"Sure can. Where are your keys?"

Her body warmed. It'd been a long time since she could rely on anyone as a friend. But for him to get her keys, he'd have to pass her bar if he left from O'Keeley's.

"With me..." she mumbled. Damn, she owed him big time.

"Good thing I'm a few blocks away. I'll be there soon." He hung up. Without reservation. Without conditions.

Just like that, Cathal dropped whatever he was doing, whoever he was with, and came to help her. Why? She knew he liked her. It wasn't more than a small infatuation, she guessed, but still, it wasn't enough to rearrange his entire day just for her.

Too bad she didn't have any plans on repaying him the way he'd probably appreciate. Life was complicated at this point. Her parents' nonstop attempts to get her to go back to her dad's distributing business. Back to Hugo. Plus, it was Cathal. Things might have shifted to a friendlier level between the two of them, but not that friendly.

"Ms. Grant?" A woman, late fifties, called her name. She held a clipboard in her hand and had a pair of glasses perched on the edge of her nose, reminding Fiona of a mean schoolteacher.

Another woman walked out beside her. She was short, round, and had a bright smile. "Mr. Thompson?"

A man down the row stood and followed her. Of course, Fiona would get the lady who huffed and crossed her arms. "Ms. Grant?"

"That's me. Are you Mickey DeLaurey?" Fiona glanced at the entrance.

"Yes, I'm Ms. DeLaurey. If you'll follow me."

Fiona exhaled with relief as Cathal walked through the glass doors. He scanned the area, finding her immediately. "Ms. DeLaurey, if you can wait one second, I need to give—"

"If you leave, you're forfeiting your appointment."

Fiona's attention snapped back to Ms. DeLaurey. She set her hands on her hips. "You've kept me waiting for over an hour. I need thirty seconds to give someone the keys to my bar so it can open on time."

"We're busy."

"Well, so am I!"

Cathal's arm landed hard across Fiona's shoulders. "Sorry I'm late." He grinned at the woman. A flat out, shit-eating grin that not even the mean schoolteacher could resist. "Are you sure you don't want me to handle this for you, darling? You seem a little tense." He squeezed her. She was aware of how close to his body she stood. The cologne she'd noticed before still subtle but suited him perfectly. It screamed confidence, and God knows the man had plenty of it.

She took a deep, calming breath. "No. I have a few additional questions to ask." She held out the keys.

He dropped his arm. "I'll see you later then." He winked. Not at her. No. He winked at poor Mrs. DeLaurey, who stood there looking a little dumbfounded.

Cathal probably had that effect on most of the women he came in contact with. That side of him didn't appeal to Fiona. Instead, those small, tiny shifts in his personality where she snagged a rare glimpse of Cathal without all the bullshit caught her attention. Serious. Pensive.

"Alright. Let's see if we can straighten this out." Fiona gave Ms. DeLaurey a wide smile.

Ms. DeLaurey watched Cathal leave. "Is that your boyfriend?"

"No. He's just a friend."

Her eyebrows shot up. "How in the hell does a man like that remain just a friend?"

She patted Ms. DeLaurey's shoulder. "It's easier than you know. I wanted to talk about my liquor license."

Ms. DeLaurey seemed to bring herself back into control. "Alright." She picked up a paper on the clipboard as she led Fiona to a small cubicle. "It seems here this is your sixth warning in a year. That's unusual."

"I agree."

"You've already had one suspension for serving to a minor."

Fiona rubbed her hands down the front of her jeans. "I

know. I have a security guard at the door. He's supposed to I.D. everyone. I don't know what happened. But I now card people a second time if they flat out look too young. And I had a long discussion with the security guard."

"Right. I see that here. Then there was a fight. Oh, it seems you've had several fights."

Fiona sighed. "Cathal. The man you just saw. Whenever there's a situation, he tends to, um, break it up." Cause it. End it.

Cathal's need to play personal Superman to every female that needs protection.

"That man?" Ms. DeLaurey glanced down the hallway as if she could still see him.

"Yes. But it has never resulted in the cops being called. Well. Except once. But that man was charged with assault on another customer. Cathal stepped in to stop the situation." And nearly crush the man's windpipe in the process.

"And what about this charge, that you're illegally filling the bottles with incorrect liquor?"

"Not true. Not at all." Fiona leaned forward. "Can you tell me who is filing these against my bar?"

Ms. DeLaurey chewed on her bottom lip a moment and looked down at the paper. "I'm really not allowed to disclose that to you." She tilted her head to the side, her eyes narrowing. "But it does seem to be the same individual."

"Is his name Hugo?"

"No." She shook her head. "It's not. That much I can say."

Fiona tapped a finger on her chin. "What do you suggest I do?"

"About what?"

"About this." She motioned to the stack of violations on the clipboard. "Someone is trying to get me to shut down."

"What about a disgruntled employee?"

Fiona shook her head. "No. I don't have any employees."

"The man that just left?"

"It's not him. These citations started happening before I even knew him." He'd never do that to her. How would he have an excuse to see her if her bar closed?

Ms. DeLaurey leaned forward, looking like she was trying to be friendly. "You mentioned your security guard." Her eyebrow twitched.

Fiona remained emotionless. Seriously?

Chuck.

"I see. Thank you for that." She rose and shook Ms. DeLaurey's hand. "I assume my bar is still allowed to operate for the time being?"

"Yes."

Fiona nodded and left the small cubicle, her mind focusing on Chuck. Why?

She walked to her bar, the mile and a half, giving her time to think. Plan. Try to figure out how to confront a man that size and hope she wouldn't wrongly accuse him.

Chuck sat outside on a chair in the shade. He halfway smiled when she stopped in front of him. "Hey. I see you gave the keys to the troublemaker."

"Cathal isn't a troublemaker." Or he was, but that wasn't the point now. "I've been down, making sure my liquor license wasn't revoked."

Chuck didn't look shocked. He casually watched someone walk by. "Oh, yeah. How'd that go?"

"Fine. One person has turned me in each time."

Chuck still didn't look at her.

Cathal appeared just inside the door, the rare, pensive expression in place.

"Do you have any idea who reported me?"

"Naw." Chuck glanced at her and then looked away again. "I'm putting all my money on the troublemaker."

Fiona rolled her eyes and set her hands on her hips. "Cathal isn't the one turning me in."

"You sound pretty defensive. Are you sleeping with the guy now?"

She tossed her hands up. "What the hell does that have to do with anything?"

"Just might cloud your judgment, is all." He linked his hands behind his head, watching her with a look she hated. A look she'd seen Hugo give her. "Do you really want to own a bar, Fiona?"

Oh. Hell. No.

She wasn't taking that shit from someone she paid. She already had to deal with it from her family. "You're fired."

Chuck stood up. "What?"

"You're fired. I think you're the one turning in all the complaints." And for a brief second, she wondered if Hugo had paid Chuck off. That was being paranoid. "I'll write you a check."

She moved past him and into her bar. Cathal wasn't in the door any longer but leaning on the wall just inside. He had the perfect angle to watch the interaction but remained concealed from Chuck. Protecting her like always.

Cathal pushed off the wall, slipping his hands into his pockets. He opened his mouth to say something, but Fiona held up her hand. "Not now."

"Fine, then." He followed her back to the bar. "But the Health Inspector showed up."

Fiona stopped. Would it ever end? "And?"

"You're fine. One minor infraction that I remedied with them here. I'll tell you about it after you pay off the jackass."

"I'm right here," Chuck said, his voice loud and echoing off the wooden walls.

Cathal didn't move from his spot, leaned against the bar, his back toward Chuck. "I know," Cathal responded.

"I've never liked you."

Cathal turned around and sat down on a barstool. "I'd have wagered that we didn't have anything in common, but I'd have lost seeing as I don't like you, either."

"You're just dragging this out for her. She's not cut out to run a bar."

Fiona couldn't stand it. "Why? Why does everyone think that?"

"I never said it," Cathal chimed in.

Chuck half-laughed. "That's because you just want in her pants."

"I've never understood that expression." His forehead wrinkled. "I don't want *in* a woman's pants. I want them gone."

Fiona stomped her foot. "Enough about my pants. Answer the question."

Chuck crossed his enormous arms, the tattoos stretching across his skin. "I've worked a lot of places. You just don't have the skills needed."

"I have a freaking business degree from an Ivy League school!" Her shout surprised her, but, damn it, she was tired of people assuming she couldn't do things. Her dad and mom. Hugo. Her old friends. The freaking security guard at her bar.

She scribbled down an amount on the check she held, no clue if it was right or not, but it was about half his typical paycheck. "Here. Take this and leave."

Chuck snatched it from her. He cut his eyes at Cathal.

Cathal waved. "Bye."

The lighthearted way he said the word almost brought a laugh out of Fiona. Chuck left, leaving them alone in the bar. She stood, staring at the empty door. Now, she had to find someone to replace him.

Fiona jumped when Cathal's hands set on her shoulders. "What—"

He squeezed the muscle and began a massage.

"Oh, my God."

He chuckled. "I once heard Selena tell Brogan that a massage was better than sex."

Fiona let her head drop forward. "At this particular moment, yes, it is."

"Just know, if the situation is ever reversed, and I have the choice, I'll take the sex over a shoulder massage. Even bad sex is better than this."

That time, Fiona did laugh. "Of course, you would."

"I'll stay tonight, work the door if you'd like."

"I owe you so much," she mumbled as his large, warm hands stroked out every knot. His thumbs pressed along the tight tendons. Between the massage and the simple feel of a man touching her, she felt a languid peace roll over her.

His hands paused. The heat from his body intensified as he moved closer, blanketing her back. If he pushed her, she wouldn't resist. Didn't want to at that one moment.

One hand slid down her back, while the other rested on her shoulder. "You don't owe me anything," he said in a low voice, his warm breath tickling her skin. His lips pressed along the curve of her neck.

She froze and closed her eyes. It felt too good for a man to touch her this way. His fingers along her hips tightened, but he didn't push the moment.

He stepped back. "You can pay me back with a shoulder massage later."

She forced her eyes open. Blinking, she cleared the haze from her mind and hoped she sounded lighthearted when she answered. "I thought you said you'd rather have sex."

"Glad you remembered." He walked to the door, dragging Chuck's chair from the sidewalk to the corner inside the entrance. "Now," he said, leaning back, his long legs stretched out in front of him. "Just shout my name if you need me. I'm going to catch a few minutes of a nap if I'm staying till closing tonight."

The warmth from the massage, his body pressing against hers, the kiss, hummed in her system. She walked back to her office, ready to make her bar a success. At that moment, she didn't give a damn what the rest of the world thought.

6

"Ladies?" Cathal rested his hands on the bar, watching the four women who stood there, giggling and whispering. Two other employees, men, leaned against the counter, looking bored but paying attention. Rarely did he feel like the oldest one in a crowd. He was just past thirty. The bartenders were all in their mid-twenties. Did five years make that much of a difference?

Or maybe they just didn't care. It wasn't their name, their livelihood on the line with the lawsuit. He didn't have the patience, not after the day from hell at work. Brogan expected him to take care of the bartenders' training to make sure they understood the course they had on serving intoxicated individuals. He hated the task but offered to do it, nonetheless. He wanted to be more involved.

After another round of snickers, Kami's eyes danced down his body.

Cathal held up his hands. Done. "Great. Glad none of you give two shits about this."

That made them all perk up. Too late.

"Brogan will conduct a follow-up discussion." He was

both satisfied and annoyed at the panic on their faces. His brother wasn't well-liked among the staff. Mainly because he demanded perfection and let them know it when they fell short. No one took Cathal seriously. It was something he'd accepted a long time ago.

After the divorce mediation today, hearing what Mrs. Cabot's asshole of a husband had done to her, his mood was still shitty when he walked into the pub.

Mara, Rian's girlfriend, cleared her throat.

Cathal turned, giving her the best smile he could. "Yes?"

"You look a little stressed." She took a sip of her drink. A plate of fries sat to the side as she rolled silverware.

"That obvious?" He walked over to where she and her friend Rachel sat. He let his smile drop as he plopped into a chair. He snagged a fry from her plate.

A picture on the wall next to him was his favorite. It was simple. Black and white. The *Hill of Tara Fairy Tree*. He'd purchased that while on a short holiday back home. It made him wish to be there now.

Away from the divorces and lawsuits. The city. He wasn't homesick often, but when things became too complicated, life seemed more relaxed back home.

Mara's hand covered his own. "Man, you worry me when you look that serious."

"Sorry."

"Don't be. You have every right to be annoyed with them. It's just, well, you look entirely different when you're not yourself, and it's a little unnerving." Her lips twisted to the side. "Especially since I'm your sister-in-law."

"You'll have to explain that a little better. How do I not look like myself?" That was an odd comment.

Rachel leaned forward. "Mara means that looking this serious and pensive, changes your face. You're a *very* good-looking man, Cathal. I'm the first one to admit it. But there's a raw edge to you when you're not trying to charm a woman out of her undies."

"Is that what I do?" That was a better description than trying to get *into* pants.

Mara winked at Rachel. "I bet if a certain red-headed bartender saw you with that serious look, she'd reconsider her feelings for you. I mean, that's how it sounded that night after Rian kissed me."

He shifted, his body alert. "Mara, darling, can you explain what you mean?" He looked between the two women. "I *need* to know anything Fiona might have said about me. It might help me crack the code."

He'd gotten closer to Fiona, but something still held her back. The pace of their relationship was a little too slow for his sanity. It was like trying to hand-feed a wild animal. He'd touched her, kissed the sweet skin along her neck, the last time they'd seen one another. She hadn't jerked away, which, honestly, shocked the hell out of him.

If he'd been prepared for consent, he'd have made a damn move then.

"She's a female, not a safe." Mara waved a fry in his direction. "After Rian kissed me in her bar, she said she wished his brother was as seductive. She also said she overcharged you for the tip for forcing her to put up with you once a week." She bit the end of the fry off. "I now see what she means."

"Seductive, eh?" Cathal hadn't assumed that about his Fiona. He couldn't walk up and trap her against the bar the way Rian had Mara. That was almost like plagiarism, stealing another man's moves. But trying to figure out Fiona was the distraction he needed after his day of divorce mediation. After listening to Mrs. Cabot relaying stories of abuse at the hands of a man who refused to give her their pet cat, had pushed his control to the limit. He needed something else to do with his brain.

Rachel took a drink of her beer before pointing it at him. "I think you should just be yourself."

"God help us all if that ever happened," he muttered.

If he could get his hands on Fiona, get her to stop all the negative thinking about him inside her pretty head, she might enjoy herself. She was a smart woman. Owned her own bar. Didn't need a man. She'd told him all those things, and he believed them to be true.

But she might not recognize that she wanted a man.

That was where he stepped in.

It'd been two days since he'd discovered the feel of her skin against his lips. It'd kept him awake most the night. Not that it was anything new for him to miss sleep, but at least he had a better memory to think about.

"You're just too pretty." Mara ate another fry.

Rian walked up from the kitchen. "Stop giving him compliments." He paused and kissed Mara lightly. "His ego is big enough already."

Rachel motioned to Cathal. "She's seen this. The charming guy with a cute accent. Any woman can spot the fact that you rarely have an empty bed a mile away." She winked. "I should know."

"Awe, but you're wrong love. I do have an empty bed. Quite often, actually."

Rian pressed another kiss against Mara's neck. "That's because any woman who saw your apartment would run for the hills. You stay at theirs."

Cathal crossed his arms. "You're not helping my case."

"You're not helping your own case. I agree with the women. You need to seduce Fiona from an entirely new angle." Rian pointed to his shirt. "Change how you dress. Order something different. Maybe try to get to know the woman before you try to sneak into her bed."

"I have gotten to know the woman. I like her."

"Then go be the real you." Mara patted his shoulder.

But Cathal didn't answer her. He and Rian watched one another for a long moment.

"It'll be fine," Rian said, his statement having more meaning than either of the women would know.

Rian's reassurance should have eased Cathal's nerves. If he let his guard down, Fiona might see right into everything he tried to hide. He wasn't proud of his past, but he'd never apologize for it. But that didn't mean he wanted to shout it around town.

Maybe he could let down his guard without divulging *everything* at once. "I'll do that." He stood. "Right now."

Mara looked at her watch. "It's only seven. Why would you go there now? And on a Monday?"

"It opens at three. I might have some time with her between the people arriving for happy hour and the nightly crowd." And he wanted to think about something other than work. Selena and Mara had both called him the "Hulk" and they weren't too far off from the truth. Certain things set him off. Today, he'd had to fight against every instinct and remain professional during the mediation.

Cathal walked to Brogan's office, not bothering to knock and ignoring his brother and Selena kissing on the sofa.

"Sure, come on in," Brogan grumbled.

"I need a spare shirt."

Brogan frowned. "Why? Did you spill something on your dress shirt?"

"No. But I'm changing things up. I need just an ordinary T-shirt."

"I have a couple I wore from the pool to the office. They're not dirty." He waved his hand toward the bathroom inside the office. "In there."

Cathal went to rummage through Brogan's old laundry. "Selena, can you come and tell me which one I look good in and don't look like myself? I'm on a mission to charm Fiona and her pants."

She walked into the room, the swell of her pregnant belly leading the way. "The black one."

He wrinkled his nose. "Black? That's Rian's color of choice. Moody artist."

"You never wear just a black shirt. Try it on." She crossed her arms and watched him undress.

"I feel like this is gym class in primary school." He made a big deal of shifting to the side so she couldn't see the front of him. It made her laugh.

Mission accomplished. He liked making Selena laugh. Figured she needed it after spending most of her time with Brogan.

He slipped on the black shirt. Although Cathal worked out daily, Brogan was the thickest of the three, neither Rian nor himself ever cared for lifting heavyweights. The T-shirt still fit. Not overly snug, but the sleeves hugged his biceps.

Cathal moved back to the center of the bathroom and held out his hands. "Well?"

Selena's eyes lit up. "Absolutely. And a pair of jeans."

"I don't have any here," he said. "Rian's are too long."

"Brogan's?"

"Isn't wearing jeans."

Selena held up a finger. "Hold on." She rushed from the room and returned a second later with a duffel bag. "These are our emergency clothes for when I go into labor. I know I packed a pair of jeans." She held up a faded pair. "These."

"I was looking for those." Brogan reached forward, but Selena blocked him.

"And you can have them after your brother wears them."

Cathal sized them up. "I guess they'll work."

"Oh, it'll work. You wear suits or dress slacks every time you've gone into Fiona's. A pair of worn jeans and a plain black shirt will make her do a double-take." She stepped forward and ran a hand through his hair, messing it up. "There. Now change."

"I will ask you to leave this time."

She rolled her eyes. "Spoilsport."

He chuckled and changed into blue jeans. They fit. Not tailored, as Brogan's rear had a little more width to it, but they'd do.

Selena grinned.

"It can't possibly be that big of a difference."

"Wanna bet?" She turned and power-walked from the room, returning a moment later with her best friend Katie, who was the fill-in shift manager for the night. Katie stopped in front of the open door to Brogan's bathroom, mouth hanging open.

She licked her lips, looking more like a dog seeing a steak than something seductive. "Did you bring me an early Christmas present?"

Selena nudged Katie. "No. Go. I just wanted an honest reaction."

Cathal smiled at Katie and shrugged as she walked away.

"Don't smile too much," Selena said.

He let the smile drop from his face. "That seems a little odd, isn't it? Wouldn't I want to seem friendly?"

"I've known you long enough to know you aren't all smiles inside. Be a little more yourself. See what happens.

Fiona seems like she can smell your bullshit from a mile away."

"I'm made up of bullshit."

"Not all of you. And—" she pointed her finger at him "—I want details."

Details? His look must have been as mortifying as he felt.

Brogan tugged Selena out of the doorway of the bathroom. "Details are not necessary. We'll talk to you later."

Cathal left Brogan's office, got four thumbs up from Mara and Rachel, and drove to Fiona's bar.

He greeted the new female security guard at the front door and walked in. Time to put the women's theory to the test.

7

Somehow, she didn't drop the bottle of Stoli she held. She couldn't formulate a sentence at the moment, but at least her hand functions were still intact. He looked sexy.

Most females who met Cathal would think that. But she'd found him to be a sweet, pompous playboy who was determined to pester her weekly and had somehow, in some strange alternate universe, managed to become a friend.

Since her friends had all chosen Hugo in their break-up, it was nice to have someone she could call that, a friend.

But why was he here, missing his liveliness? His smile. She checked her watch. It wasn't Friday or Saturday, his usual days. It wasn't ten-thirty, his usual time. And he wasn't wearing something that probably cost more than clothing should cost.

She licked her lips as her mouth felt dry from hanging open. His low-slung jeans weren't fabricated to look faded and worn. Not like the kind you pulled off the shelf at the department store. They'd been worked in, faded from repeated washes. Did he do manual labor?

Setting the bottle of vodka on the shelf, she wiped her

hands on the towel, which hung from her back pocket. Suddenly, she wanted to touch her hair and check her appearance. But it was Cathal. Someone who she'd relied on too much lately, and it had obviously clouded her judgment. He fit into the friend category. The end.

Not into the category of someone who she wanted to climb all over. Who knew that was even a damn category?

She turned around. He watched her. His blue eyes were dark. Not sad. But not happy like they usually were. Intense. Focused.

His gaze flicked down her body and back up as she crossed to him, stealing her breath with it. He didn't smile. His lips formed a tight line. The muscle along his jaw jumped like he gritted his teeth together for some reason. What could the happy-go-lucky Cathal have to stress over?

"Hi. I wasn't expecting to see you." Good. That just let him know she expected to see him. Which she did, but not for the reasons skipping through her sex-starved mind.

He sat down, interlacing his fingers, and watched her another long moment before speaking. "Can I have a beer?"

"Beer? No whiskey?"

He shook his head. "A little early for that."

She felt her lips twitch. "I would have bet money to hear you say that. I figure you drank whiskey with your cereal in the mornings."

He smirked, but his voice remained lower than usual. "Only when I've stayed up all night."

How did he have this much hold over her? She knew better than to get involved with a flirt like him. Walking in on her fiancé and maid of honor the night before her wedding eliminated her desire for men like him. But she hated sticking him in that one place in her mind.

He was reliable and kind. He helped his brothers. He

helped her without complaint. She knew there was more to him, but to see him looking the opposite of how she'd pinned him in her mind threw her world into a frenzy.

"What's wrong?" she asked.

"Nothing," he replied. "Long day."

"Why didn't you go to your own bar? I assume you drink for free there?"

"I don't drink for free, but that's not the reason. It's because my family is there. My brothers and their women." He lifted a shoulder, the black shirt shifting across his muscles. When did he get those? "That's a lot of people who think they know all about you. Your history."

"And they don't?" She pulled out a Bud Lite from the cooler and took the top off, sliding it to him. "I always assumed you were close with your family since you all owned the pub."

"Oh, they know the history." He took a drink. For a strange reason, she expected him to cough or grimace because it wasn't his beloved whiskey. But he didn't. "They don't always grasp the full impact it had."

She suddenly understood what exactly he meant. Everyone in her family knew about the cheating. The called-off engagement. They'd returned hundreds of wedding gifts. But they didn't know how it'd changed her. Deep down, it'd altered her DNA. What she wanted. What she needed. What she'd put up with.

"I get it," she heard herself say.

His eyes narrowed as if he tried to see if she were lying. "You do?"

"Yes." She shook her head. "But I'm on this side of the bar. That means you spill your guts. Not the other way around."

He smiled. Not a sexy, in her face kind. But easy and

amused. He ran a hand through his hair, again, the muscles he'd hidden hard to ignore.

She reached back and grabbed a beer.

"You don't usually drink," he said.

"I need one now, apparently." Something to relax her because he had done nothing but wound her tighter and tighter.

He held up his bottle, and she touched hers to his.

"Now, spill."

"My beer?"

She half-laughed. "No, smart ass. What happened that made you so melancholy?"

He tilted his head to the side. "Do you know what I do for a living?"

"You own O'Keeley's. You work there."

"Yes, I do. I work when I'm needed, and I'm in the way otherwise." He took another sip. "I'm a lawyer, Fiona."

"Like, a serious one?" She grimaced. "I'm sorry. That came out wrong. I didn't expect you to have a real job. A hard job." She took a long drink of beer to get her mind straight. "An adult job. No. Sorry-"

"It's fine. I know everyone sees me as the lazy younger brother."

"I wouldn't say you were lazy."

He grinned, a little evidence that he really was the same man that came in every Friday. "You would if you saw my apartment."

She didn't want him back to flirting like he usually did. This side of Cathal fascinated her. "Back to being a lawyer. Do you work at a firm or for yourself?" Why was she asking so many questions? Would he think she was as easy as the other women he dated? She hoped not. She wanted to know him, the real him. The man who'd give up both weekend nights to give his brother and pregnant sister-in-law a weekend off. *That's* the man she wanted to know.

"What's got you down now?" He asked. "Does me being a lawyer make you that sad?"

"It obviously makes you sad."

He nodded. "That's right. I'm on the wrong side of the bar to ask questions. Seeing that I'm a serious, adult lawyer with a real, hard job, I sometimes have to take cases with serious issues. Certain things, they, well, make me angry."

"So, I've noticed. Are you a criminal attorney?"

"I've done that, but I don't enjoy the trial bit. The case I had today was a divorce case. Two children. The husband is fighting to keep everything." He turned the rest of his beer up, draining it. She automatically pulled him another one from the cooler.

"Divorce makes you angry?" Why wouldn't he get to the point? She was desperate to know what could make this man switch from one extreme to the other and make her entire world look different. To make her care and want to be the woman to make it right again.

"Of course, that does. But it's this particular situation. Every time I've fought in your bar, do you know why?"

She did. He couldn't sit by and ever let a man lay a hand on a woman. It went far beyond the Superman routine.

"The first time I met you, you almost killed a man in my bar for grabbing your friend."

"Selena."

"Selena? I don't think I knew that was your brother's wife."

"Yes. And that's the anger I mean."

Rage. It wasn't just someone mad that night. He had an unsettling level of anger that she could never reconcile with the man that came in every Friday, trying to sweet-talk her into his bed. Violent. She'd told him as much, but after the past months, she'd changed her mind. He wasn't violent. Not by nature.

He rubbed his temple with his free hand, gripping his beer with the other. "I hadn't even planned to get into this tonight."

"Well, you're in, and I'm curious. You were talking about the anger?"

"With a name like Fiona and all that red hair and an obvious affinity for gossip, how are you not Irish?"

She bit her bottom lip to keep from the harsh laugh that wanted to burst out of her mouth. "I don't know. Maybe I am."

He took a sip of his new beer. "Alright. Full disclosure?"

"Please."

"You'll probably kick me out of your bar and never speak to me again after this, but here it goes." He leaned back and clasped his hands in his lap. "I was eighteen and dating a girl. We'd been fairly serious for a few months, I'd say." He looked away and took a breath.

Fiona ducked underneath the edge of the bar to stand beside him. He looked so lost for a second, she wanted to reach out to him, but she didn't. Couldn't interrupt his story.

He finally brought his gaze back to her. God, he was gorgeous with his dark expression. Dangerous, but she knew he'd never hurt her.

"I went to pick her up. She worked at her da's shop in the small town where we lived. She closed at night. It was dark early that day. Almost mid-winter. I went around back. And found her, stripped bare, huddled against the wall."

Fiona heard herself gasp. She set her hand on his shoulder, trying to offer him comfort. His voice had gone flat. Cold. She suppressed the shiver that came from thinking of the girl.

"Her face was bruised. Lip split. She looked up at me, and I knew then what'd happened. Then I heard it." He tilted his head to the side like he heard it again. "A closing of a door inside the shop. A glass breaking. The bloody bastard was still in there. Robbing them."

Based on his reaction the night the man grabbed Selena, she assumed he didn't stop and call the police. She squeezed his shoulder.

"I took my shirt off and gave it to her. She was shaking her head 'no' for me not to go in there, but I couldn't stop myself. That was part of my defense later—that I was half out of my mind and wasn't making rational choices. But I knew what I was doing. Knew what I was going to do before I even pushed open the back door. And I came face-to-face with the man who'd raped her."

Fiona ran a hand up and down his spine, but he didn't seem to notice. He looked so lost. And the ghost of the rage he'd described flickered in his eyes. She hadn't expected this intense emotion from him. Most people came into her bar pissed off at their work because of their boss or a coworker. No, Cathal had something deep inside that he didn't often acknowledge.

"I fought him. I was smaller back then. Thinner. I couldn't have done what I did to Simmons in your bar that night. For the man, I'm not sure that was a good thing or not. I might have ended him quicker."

She swallowed. She knew his answer before she even asked the question. "Ended him?"

He looked up at her, his eyes clear of the pain and anguish. "I killed him."

She didn't know how to respond, so she stayed silent as

she looked down at him, sitting on the barstool. He sat in the same spot he always did, but everything had changed.

He shifted, his hands gripping her waist as he tugged her to step in between his legs and face him. A deep breath lifted his shoulders.

She wanted to be closer. Touch him. Comfort him. When had those feelings developed?

His hands tightened. "We fought. I used everything my brothers had taught me. Every item in that store I could make into a weapon, I did. He had a knife, and at one point, it turned away from being about my girlfriend and to survival. That was also part of my defense. Kill or be killed. Eventually, at some point, the guard arrived. She'd run to another store and alerted them. But they couldn't pull me off. Not then. I kept hammering at the man even though he was still. No. It took Brogan to pull me off. He'd been at the bank, a few doors down when it'd happened." He sighed and looked up at her.

She ran a hand through his brown hair. "Were you arrested?"

He watched her, intent on something. Her reaction? He didn't scare her. At one point, after the first incident in her bar, she thought he was prone to fighting. He'd gotten into enough scuffles in her bar over the past few months to prove that he had a defensive nature, but Cathal wasn't dangerous. Not like she'd initially thought.

"We left for America after I was out of prison."

She wasn't sure if he pulled her closer or she stepped on her own, but in a blink, his hands wrapped around her waist and hers around his neck. How? How could everything between them shift in a matter of minutes?

She swallowed down the question, forcing herself to go along with what he needed. Because she needed it just as much. It'd been a long time since a man held her that way. Like he needed *her*. And for that one moment, Fiona wanted to be that woman for Cathal. Because she knew he'd never opened like this to all the other one-night stands, he'd had over the years.

This was where their friendship intersected with intense physical attraction.

"How did your divorce case bring all this back up?"

"The wife told me today her husband abused her. Physically. Sexually. That when she'd finally left after the last time, he hit her son." He swallowed. "And then I got to meet the bastard. Sit across from the man as he snickered and claimed that his wife wasn't entitled to anything. That she deserved to be left without a penny." He closed his eyes. His hands fisted behind her back. "And not slam him face-first into the conference table."

Did he expect that to scare her away? Fiona brushed her thumb along his temple, and his eyes opened. "I'm sorry. That must be very hard to live with. And you were right earlier. No one truly knows what it feels like to go through that and still have it resurface."

He didn't speak. Slowly, his hands relaxed along her lower back. "I came here tonight, hoping to convince you to finally come out with me. I needed the distraction. I changed how I dressed, what I ordered, and here I am. You're in my arms." He rose, their bodies brushing together in the motion, but he didn't drop his hands. And she didn't either. She couldn't tear herself away. She wanted him for the distraction as well.

"I hadn't planned on having to lay open the darkest part of my soul to get you."

He was wrong. So wrong. She skimmed the back of her fingers along his cheek, a little rough with his five o'clock shadow. "That might be the darkest part of your past, Cathal, but that's not what's in your soul. You protect people. You make them laugh. Smile." She gently pulled his head down. "Your soul isn't dark."

She kissed him. Nothing more than a simple sweep of her lips over his. But the light touch set her brain firing in four hundred different ways. Questioning why she'd done it. Wondering why she'd fought her attraction for so long. Wishing she could take away that desolation in his eyes. She pulled back.

The intensity in his gaze pierced straight through to her heart. His arms tightened around her. She half expected him to crack a joke. That would have been typical. The charming man. The one everyone else saw. But he didn't.

Cathal slid his fingers into her hair, cup her cheek, and pulled her tight against his body that felt on fire. "I need more," he whispered as his head lowered to hers.

She expected a rough, solid kiss, but instead, received soft lips that coaxed hers apart with a gentle breath.

The taste of beer, cool on his tongue, made her need more as well. More than she could give standing at the end of the bar with a handful of customers.

He kept the kiss relaxed.

She released the back of his shirt when she realized she'd fisted it in her hands. She knew then she'd end up in his bed if she weren't careful. Her life had too many loose ends to take a fun tumble with Cathal. This kiss was nearly nine months in the making, but it was all they could have.

"Fiona?"

No. Why did she hear—

She pulled back and blinked up at Cathal.

"Is this what you're doing now?" The man's voice said again.

She leaned to the side. What the hell? There he stood. Her dad.

"Dad! Hi!" She tried to leave Cathal's arms, but he made it difficult. His lips tilted up in amusement. "Don't you dare laugh," she muttered.

"I would never." He finally let her go. He turned around and held out his hand. "Hi, I'm Cathal O'Keeley. It's a pleasure to meet you."

No. No. No. Why was he introducing himself? None of that was supposed to have happened to begin with.

Her dad hadn't changed, he crossed his arms, refusing to shake Cathal's hand.

Cathal's head cocked to the side, and he let his hand drop. "I see. Well, I'll assume then the pleasure is only on this side of the introduction."

"I thought you told me you were working through things. We let you have your little bar and throw your tantrum, but kissing other men? Young lady, do you realize this might ruin your engagement?"

8

F iona had made the first move. Cathal kept telling himself as she and her father argued at the other end of the bar. He hadn't encroached on another man's territory. She didn't wear a ring. She'd come to him. She kissed him.

But an engagement?

It'd looked to be news to her. She didn't consider herself engaged if he were to bet on it. And he immediately hated whoever it was. Because right or wrong, he wanted Fiona for himself.

She looked at Cathal. He almost lifted his hand to wave and try to bring a smile to her sullen expression, but her focus snapped back to her da at whatever he said.

A man sat down on the opposite corner from him. Tailored suit. Perfectly combed blond hair. Thin frame. Money. He could almost smell it on the guy. And Fiona watched him with contempt.

Good.

A certain level of wealth Cathal would never compete with. The more general kind he could. He had money. Rich compared to how he grew up. Money didn't intimidate him.

The man glanced Cathal's direction. "Can I help you?"

Cathal shook his head slowly. "Probably not. Did you want anything to drink?"

"Do you work here?" He glanced down at Cathal's clothes. "Taking a break or wasting Fiona's money? Doesn't surprise me. She doesn't know how to run a bar."

Cathal made an elaborate movement to look at his watch. It was either that or kick the stool out from underneath the fellow and hope his face hit the bar and knocked out a tooth or two.

"My shift is about to start." He rose and ducked underneath the bar. Was this the man engaged to Fiona? She didn't seem so happy about whoever he was. Her eyes widened when she saw Cathal start mixing a drink. Another person came up to the bar, and Cathal served them as well.

He could handle the bar. That was about the only aspect of O'Keeley's he could do without his brothers watching over him. That and handling their legal troubles. They seemed to rely on him, and he appreciated their confidence.

Her dad pounded his hand on the bar and shouted something.

The hair on the back of Cathal's neck rose. He paused in scooping ice, trying like hell to keep his shoulders relaxed. Anyone, even her father, shouting at Fiona, pushed him to his limit.

Her dad slapped his hand on the bar again, and Fiona jumped.

Slowly, with as much control as he could muster, Cathal set the glass in his hand down and took a step their direction. No man would intimidate Fiona while he was around. He didn't care if it were her da or the President.

"I wouldn't get in the middle of that if I were you, dude,"

the blond guy stated. "She can be a bit thickheaded sometimes."

Cathal took a deep breath. It never really worked to calm him down, but everyone on television did it. He took long, slow steps in their direction. Even without the fantastic kiss, he'd have come to her defense. He liked Fiona. Liked the woman. Her attitude. Her determination to make her bar a success. The way her jeans clung to her ass. He'd noticed that last part every week he visited.

"Did you need something?" Her dad said. "I don't see how this conversation involves you."

Fiona's head hung down. Her hands were in fists, and her cheeks were red.

Cathal dropped his arm over her shoulders. She stiffened but didn't pull away. He'd protect her the best way he knew how without his fists. "I don't like it when anyone, including her da, yells at my girlfriend. I assume you remember how to speak with a proper inside voice, as my ma would call it."

Her dad didn't seem to appreciate the reminder. He slapped his hand on the bar again. Fiona jerked.

Cathal held her tighter. Fiona went toe-to-toe with him whenever he fed her some of his typical horseshit. Why didn't she give that attitude back to her da? Stand up to the man. Shout back. Do something besides stand there and take it.

"Boyfriend? You were supposed to have six months to give you and Hugo time to settle everything. It's been a year, and *now* you have a boyfriend?"

Hugo. It even sounded pretentious. The man in question rose from the end of the bar. Ah, he didn't like someone touching Fiona. Too bad, she just slipped her hand around Cathal's waist. Her chin came up.

A beat of pride welled up in his chest. She wasn't upset or scared like he'd thought. She was all out fuming mad-as-hell and trying to keep it inside. He assumed if she were a cartoon, she'd have steam rolling out of her pretty ears.

"Why is he holding you?" Hugo crossed his arms. It was comforting, knowing that he didn't even have to worry about a fight with this man. Granted, not everything in the world ended up coming to blows. It just seemed as of lately, the fighting for him and his brothers had amped itself up again. Women were always the cause.

Fiona's fingers tightened on his side. "He's my boyfriend." Yes. He could easily play that role for her.

"But we're engaged," Hugo said, not even looking upset. Odd. If Cathal had a girl he considered his fiancé hold onto another man, he might be a bit more peeved than Hugo appeared to be. Hugo just looked—bored.

"You ended the engagement, Hugo."

He shook his head. "I'm telling you, what you thought you saw, didn't happen. I've forgiven you for how everything turned out, and I want you to come home." He looked at Cathal. "To *our* house."

"I stopped paying the rent on your apartment." Her dad pursed his lips together like he was digging in for a fight. "You have no choice but to come back."

She cocked a hip out and planted her hand on it. "Dad, plenty of people don't rely on their parents for income. I make enough to get by off the bar. I don't need you and mom paying for everything."

"Then you can give me the keys to your car." He held out his hand.

She dug into her pocket and slapped them in his palm. Cathal saw the BMW key before her da pocketed them. Fiona had tried to make a go of it on her own with the bar.

And now her da had demonstrated in every way possible that she couldn't do it.

She wasn't defeated. Not yet.

"It's okay." Cathal kissed her temple, earning an extra harsh glare from her da. "We talked about her moving in with me anyway. And seeing how my apartment is around the block from here, she can either use my car or walk."

"Your car? She loved her BMW," Hugo replied with a smirk.

Her chin kicked out a notch. "I'll be happy to drive Cathal's car. I'm not a snob like you."

"What does he drive? That crappy, little car sitting out front?"

Her mouth opened and then closed. No. She wouldn't know what he drove.

"I don't guess you've ever asked what type of Mercedes it is, have you?"

Her head shot up. "No. I never did."

"It's the SL 550 Roadster you passed walking into the bar." He enjoyed Hugo's sudden shock. Her dad didn't seem as impressed.

"Young lady-"

"Stop calling me that."

"Then start acting like an adult."

She stomped her foot, narrowly missing Cathal's. "I'm thirty-one. I own a bar. I pay taxes. I only let you and mom pay for my apartment because you didn't want me to live where I could afford it. I'll be happy to let you take it all back."

Her dad shook his head. "You're unreasonable. You heard what he said. You didn't see what you thought you did."

Fiona crossed her arms. "Don't try to brainwash me. Mom saw it, too."

Cathal pressed a kiss to the top of her head, dying to know what everyone "saw" that they kept mentioning. So far, he figured at one point, Fiona and old Hugo were engaged, she'd called it off when she saw *something,* and now Hugo is back to win his bride back. And doing a right shitty job of it. Who brings the girl's da with them to help out?

Cathal's phone rang from his back pocket. He pulled it out. "It's that case I told you about earlier." He kissed her lips, enjoying the surprise that popped into her eyes. He could pretend to be her boyfriend for a little bit. Especially with the perk of touching her. "Don't let Hugo here steal you back before I return." He winked.

She barked out a harsh laugh.

He answered his phone, walking a few feet away. "Cathal O'Keeley."

A crying woman greeted him. Her words were unintelligible, but he recognized the voice.

"Mrs. Cabot. What's wrong."

"He came by here."

The fear in her words iced his blood.

"What do you mean he came by there?" He gripped the edge of the bar—grounding him to something substantial. God, his restraint had been jerked around today.

"He came here."

"Did he touch you?" He tried to control his voice, but he couldn't. More crying. "Mrs. Cabot, did he hurt you?"

Fiona's hand covered his. "Calm down," she demanded in a soft, firm way.

Her touch did more than he'd expected. It soothed him. "Call the guard, I mean the police. Call them. File a report. We'll handle this in the morning. Come down to the office."

"Ah...Alright."

"And for goodness sake, lock the damn door."

"I will." She hung up.

Fiona rubbed a hand up and down his back like she'd done when he'd told her his story. She stepped around, facing him, nothing but open concern. No panic.

His jaw clenched. He could do this with Fiona, let out the thoughts battering into his brain. She hadn't pushed him away before. "I want to go over there."

"But you know that isn't the best thing to do. She needs to call the police, as you said." Her calm, rational voice seemed like an antidote to his aggression.

Cathal pinched the bridge of his nose. "I'm going to be honest with you, Fiona. I'm not a good bet. Even as a fake boyfriend. I know what you think about my past being in my past, but it could happen again." He opened his eyes. He saw a flash of disappointment. He cupped her cheek. "But I'm going to help you through this shite with your family. I meant it. I have a spare bedroom and everything."

"Thanks. I may need it for a little bit." She smiled. "I still get to drive your car, right?"

"Absolutely."

She moved a fraction closer and wrapped her arms around his neck. "And the rest?"

"Whatever you need, Fiona." He leaned down, capturing her lips with his. How had his entire world just turned over on its damned head?

9

F iona waited by the front door, anxious to get the entire thing over with. She'd packed up everything in her small, luxury apartment. Most of the furniture she'd send to storage or her parents could handle. The only things she planned on taking to Cathal's place were clothing and a few personal items. She'd packed and unpacked the pictures of her parents. It felt petty, letting this come between them, possibly never reconciling again, but they'd put themselves in that position.

They'd taken Hugo's side along with all her friends. She still didn't know why. Really, the "why" didn't matter. They'd chosen him over her. Hugo worked in her dad's distributing company. The same business that her dad claimed she'd been groomed to take over. And she'd been willing to go along with his plans. She and Hugo would run the company when he retired.

But even if she forgave Hugo, made amends with her parents, she didn't want that life. It'd been fake and lonely. Her friends had disappeared, and she hadn't tried to make many new ones. Being alone suited her.

Now, she had Cathal in her life. Strange that the man who'd irritated her for nearly a year was now her boyfriend. *Fake* boyfriend. Although it was hard to remember, they had a superficial relationship. The friendship they'd developed over the past few weeks shifted quickly into something more.

Cathal hadn't asked any questions about Hugo. After her dad's surprise visit, he'd stayed the rest of the night, helped her behind the bar, drove her home, and kissed her goodnight. Damn, the man could kiss.

But she'd draw the line there. Her life was too complicated to get physically involved with a man like Cathal. He wasn't a jerk like Hugo, but they were somewhat similar. Charming. Dated dozens of women. Because Hugo had. Before her, and then during this "break" they were on. Her dad could scream and shout all he wanted to about her dating Cathal, not that they were, but his own "prodigy" had definitely partaken in plenty of women.

But then again, there was always a double standard with her dad.

That's why her dad had pretended that nothing had happened at the wedding. Like she didn't see her maid of honor's underwear tossed on the floor while she rolled around on the bed. The one thing she wished she'd do differently was to make a scene. Throw something. Let everyone in the world know what'd happened—it wasn't between the two of them and her and her mom.

Her upbringing had prevented her. Quiet and reserved. Controlled. Act with class and dignity.

If she had a do-over in her life, that one moment would be it. She'd have chased after Hugo and verbally beat the hell out of him. Then maybe, if she'd had a larger audience, she wouldn't have lost all her friends in the process when everyone blamed her for not believing the snake.

But did she really want friends that would walk away so easily?

The doorbell rang, and Fiona straightened her shoulders. She and Cathal kissed two days ago, and she hadn't seen him since. He'd offered her his apartment and pretended to be her boyfriend, but what next? She couldn't lose her heart and then always wonder if he found another woman. But maybe, for a short time, she'd enjoy the company of a man. The companionship.

She opened the door. But it wasn't Cathal. "Can I help you?"

"I'm Brogan. Cathal's oldest brother. I'm here to assist in the move."

She glanced behind him. "But, where's Cathal?"

"He's on the way. The mediation case ran long. He said you'd know what case he was talking about." He clapped his hands together. "Now, I can load up some of the smaller boxes until he gets here, have him help me with the big things."

"I don't need big things moved. It's all going to storage."

Brogan nodded. "Found a furnished place, right?"

Fiona crossed her arms; a nagging feeling stiffened her spine. "Cathal didn't tell you where I was moving, I'm guessing."

Brogan rose with a cardboard box in his hands. "He didn't tell me much of anything. His case has had him absent from O'Keeley's. Normally, he's at the restaurant, lazing around, but we haven't seen him. Why? Where are you moving to?"

She swallowed. "In with Cathal."

Brogan, bless him, managed not to drop the box he held although his eyes widened into saucers. "You're moving in...on purpose? Have you, uh, seen the state of his apartment?"

"No, but it's a long story, and I'm grateful he's giving me a place until I can get back on my own feet again." But his reaction worried her.

"Fiona?"

She grimaced at the sound of Hugo's voice calling from the end of the hallway. "I'm sorry," she whispered to Brogan. "But the man coming up here is the ex-fiancé that I found knocking boots with my maid of honor."

Brogan's mouth formed an "o" as his eyebrows shot up.

"And he and my dad are trying to get me to go back to him. Cathal pretended to be my boyfriend, my dad took my apartment and my car, and he won't just leave me alone."

"Cathal, your ex, or your dad?"

"My ex and my dad."

"So, you and Cathal are or are not together?" Brogan glanced over his shoulder as Hugo came into view.

She hesitated. "We're complicated."

"You sound like my wife. Alright. I'll play along. It sounds like something Cathal would get himself into."

Her shoulders relaxed. "Thanks. Really." She took a breath to control her features. "Hugo? Why are you here?"

He pointed at Brogan. "Is he another-" he did the air quotes "-boyfriend? You didn't fool me, Fiona. I came to move you back home."

"I'm not going to your house with you."

"We bought the house together."

"No. You picked it out. You picked out the paint. The kitchen tiles. The ugly carpet. All that was you. And if I didn't find out about your extracurricular activities, you allowed me to stay there."

"Your parents want us to be together. And I do, too."

Brogan shifted in front of her, his broad shoulders blocking her ex. "I think she just told you no." Did the protective streak run in Cathal's family?

"What? Are you related to the other guy at the bar?" He shook his head. "I don't understand you, Fiona. Your choices of men to associate with are a little disconcerting."

"Good. That's good. Maybe you'll leave me alone."

Cathal appeared in the doorway. He'd worn a dress shirt and a pair of slacks. His top button was unbuttoned, and his tie was loosened. He shouldn't make her pulse race. Not when their relationship was a sham from the get-go.

"Why, if it isn't old Hugo." He slapped him hard on the back. Hugo flinched. "Brogan, have you been introduced to Fiona's ex, Hugo?"

"We were just getting to know each other. I'm going to load up the smaller boxes." He raised his eyebrows. "I don't think you've properly greeted your girlfriend."

Cathal's eyes lit up like a kid on Christmas morning. Flattering and terrifying at the same time. Fiona had to keep from taking a step backward. She had a brief taste of regret for doing this—getting him involved. But he seemed to enjoy the pretense. For her, it was about to be the longest few weeks of her life.

"Hi, Cathal," she said with an awkward wave.

Cathal slapped Hugo on the back again. "You might want to turn away. Or, even better, you're welcome to leave." He nudged Hugo over, stepping to Fiona and sliding a hand along the base of her neck, into her hair. And he kissed her. Without asking permission. Without the slightest hesitation.

She gasped. His dominance in his kiss shocked her. A man had never kissed her that way.

The kiss wasn't like the few they shared before. It wasn't the slow simmer that made her wish she was the kind of girl that fell into bed without a second thought. No. This rocked her deep the minute their lips touched.

He kissed her with something primal inside. Like he was starving, and she was the only way to satisfy him. Hell, she wished she could.

Hugo snapped out, "give me a break," but Cathal didn't listen to him or seem to care.

She wanted the passion for real. They were attracted to each other, but this kiss was for show. For Hugo to report back to her parents that she'd, in fact, moved on.

Cathal leaned away. "Damn, but my Fiona knows how to kiss."

Her face grew warm.

He lowered his voice; no way Hugo could hear. "And I enjoy knowing I'm the one making you blush."

He didn't mean it. She wished he did, but his fundamental nature was comprised of nothing but pure, sexy charm. He couldn't help it. She leaned to the side and looked at Hugo.

"We're moving today. Please, leave. I know what I saw-"

Cathal held up his hand. "About that. I never did get the full story."

It was Hugo's turn to blush, his cheeks turning ruddy. "I don't want to get into it."

Cathal watched her a long, pensive moment. His fists tightened before he relaxed his hands, wiggling his fingers once.

She slipped her hand into his, squeezing it. "It's nothing like that. I promise. Let's just say he enjoyed my maid of honor in our honeymoon suite the afternoon *before* the wedding."

The tension rushed out of his body. She saw it leave. He was no less angry and sent Hugo a mean glare, but it wasn't that edge of being violent. He could control himself. She wished he saw that.

"I'm telling you-"

But Cathal didn't let Hugo finish. "Goodbye, Hugo." He nudged him out the door and shut it in his face.

Fiona grinned and threw her arms around Cathal. "No one else ever takes my side on that."

"You mean both Hugo and your da keep telling you that you didn't see it happen? That's ridiculous. What did your maid of honor say?"

"She admitted to it at first and then backtracked. I wish I could see her bank account. I have no doubt they paid her off." Wren had been her best friend. For all Fiona knew, Wren and Hugo still saw each other, although she'd be shocked if anyone ever admitted it.

"Why is your da so set on your marrying Hugo?"

She looked away. "I'd rather not get into that right now." She'd keep her emotional baggage packed away in her suitcase for the time being.

Cathal kissed her temple. "That's fine. I'll get to pester you about it at my place."

Brogan opened the door and walked into the apartment.

"You know," Cathal began, setting his arm around Fiona's shoulders. "I'm seeing someone now, so you might need to knock."

Fiona laughed. She couldn't help it with the deadpan way he'd announced their unusual relationship.

Brogan picked up another box. "Yeah, and you haven't forgotten to lock your door since Ma caught you with your first girl." He sent a flirty smirk at Fiona, and she immediately saw the family resemblance. "Welcome to the family, even if it's only temporary."

Temporary. She'd accepted those terms and would have to get used to them.

10

Brogan stopped in the doorway to Cathal's apartment. "You cleaned."

Fiona stopped a few steps inside and half-laughed. "Cleaned? This is clean?" She looked at Cathal. Was she scared? "Sorry." She made a face somewhere between a grimace and an apology. She shouldered her purse and then smoothed a hand down the front of her purple T-shirt. He liked her wearing purple. It brought out the blue in her fairy eyes. "I really appreciate you letting me stay."

Cathal surveyed the room. He'd cleaned. Some. The kitchen sink was empty. He'd tossed his laundry, clean and dirty, into his bedroom, and closed the door. Wiped down the table. Swept the floors. Overall, he thought it looked pretty decent compared to how he usually lived.

"Follow me." He led her across the floor, past a few boxes he'd never unpacked since moving to Atlanta from college. He'd spent most of his evenings the past two days in her guest room, even having Mara come over early that morning and bring some new sheets and a spread for the bed. He wanted Fiona comfortable.

He opened the door. The room felt bright and happy. Mara had left the window shades pulled up, bringing in extra light. The cheery spread on the bed was white with small pink flowers blooming over a green vine. More pillows than he thought necessary were stacked at the headboard.

It even smelled nice. Something that resembled cupcakes.

He owed Mara a little more than a text telling her thanks.

Fiona, again, paused in the doorway.

"You have a hard time entering a room." Cathal pushed her forward.

"The first time was out of shock. And now, this is out of shock, too. You didn't have to do all this for me." She turned in a circle. "It's so pretty in here."

"That would be Rian's Mara that helped."

Brogan gave him a thumbs-up behind Fiona's back. "I'm going to leave her boxes right outside this door."

"Oh, thank you, Brogan, for helping." She smiled. "My own family has been horrible, and a fake boyfriend and his brother rescued me."

"No thanks needed, and I suspect you could've rescued yourself based on what Cathal has said, but I'm always glad to help. I need to get back to the restaurant and make sure my wife isn't dead on her feet. I'll see you around." Brogan left, closing the front door behind him.

"So-" Cathal rubbed his hands together "-do you want help with your unpacking?"

"No. I'll do it later. Right now, if it's alright, I might take a nap. I stayed up all night, boxing up my life, basically, and I won't be worth a damn to make it to closing tonight."

"You do not have to ask permission for anything in this apartment. If you want to sleep, sleep. Eat, eat. Laundry, throw some of my briefs in the wash as I always seem to be out." He'd not slept himself, and the idea of a nap, with Fiona, suited him. He only survived on naps, typically. Deep sleep, in the dark and silence, always left him disturbed and unsettled. "I'll be back in a moment."

He left to change. Sweatpants and an undershirt. By the time he returned, Fiona was already curled up on the edge of the bed, her hands tucked under her cheek.

He climbed onto the bed beside her.

She jerked awake. "Cathal-"

Pulling her into his arms, he'd savor having someone...no, having *Fiona* there with him, even if for a little bit. The cupcake smell of the room faded as he breathed in against her hair. Honeysuckles that was uniquely Fiona.

She made a little huff of annoyance.

"Be quiet. You're keeping me awake."

She smiled against his chest. "Do we need to set the alarm?"

"Here." He tapped his watch, setting the alarm for two hours. Not that he planned to sleep that long. Then, he turned off all other notifications so they wouldn't wake her up. "Done."

She snuggled back against his chest and yawned. "We really shouldn't get used to this relationship. The past two days have been emotional for us both, but we know we'd kill each other eventually."

He didn't respond. He'd never grow tired of Fiona, but he agreed it wouldn't last. It never did. He couldn't take that chance.

～

CATHAL'S WATCH MADE A SOFT, beeping noise in the dim

room. They'd shifted at some point during their nap, his body curved around Fiona like he protected her from something. The smell of him enveloped her the same way. Three days ago, she'd have thought him climbing into bed to take a nap was a ploy to get her naked.

That was before she understood him a little better. Or a lot better. His past had shaped him into the superficial, flirtatious man that didn't take relationships seriously. And now, surprisingly, she hated that for him. He'd protected his girlfriend and had paid a sharp consequence—not a set jail sentence.

Cathal had sentenced himself for the rest of his life.

He shifted, touching his watch and silencing the alarm. His lips pressed against a spot behind her ear. "That was too short. I haven't slept that well in a while."

Her body reacted, stretching out along the length of him, her head tilting to the side.

She gave in, allowing his hand to slip underneath her shirt along her stomach. He kissed her neck. Each press of his lips shot through her body. It'd be so easy to stay partially asleep, pretending this was a fantastic sex dream with a man she no doubt knew exactly what to do in bed.

His hand stroked along her ribcage until his fingertips brushed along the underneath side of her breast.

He'd stopped breathing, the natural rise and fall of his chest stalling.

"Fiona?" He skimmed his fingers to the other breast, caressing it the same way. It'd been so long since a man touched her.

But she'd regret having sex with him like this.

"We can't do that, Cathal. It will complicate everything." And she wasn't ready for another heartbreak. She sat up, avoiding his eye contact. "I'm going to take a shower."

"First, you shoot me down. Then you tease me." Cathal knelt on the bed behind her, kissing her one last time along the side of her neck before climbing off. "Fine then. I meant it when I told you that you could use my car. I can steal Brogan's or Rian's car if necessary. Preferably Rian's car as Brogan's looks like a da car already."

"I really appreciate it. I hope to be out of your way in a couple weeks."

Cathal shrugged and turned to leave. "You're a fine woman to have in my way, so you won't be hearing any complaints from me."

He said that now, but when it dawned on him that having a girlfriend, even a fake one, meant his normal activities might be a little sequestered, he might not want her taking up his spare bedroom.

She took a quick shower in the guest bathroom. It was marginally clean. She'd make time in the future and deep clean it. If she was staying there, rent-free, then the least she could do was help.

Her shower helped clear her head, and she dried off and dressed quickly. She'd brought her clothes with her into the bathroom. She'd seen too many movies where the heroine leaves in her towel and ends up in the hero's bed.

And since her dream had put her in that bed, it was better that she leaves the bathroom with her bra on, shirt buttoned, and jeans zipped.

Cathal stood in the kitchen, without a shirt. She couldn't see his lower body. "You better be wearing pants."

He turned, a piece of carrot sticking out of his mouth. He crunched on it and took her in with a flirtatious, heated gaze. "I can take them off if you'd like."

"No!"

He grinned. "Fine then. I was eating a snack before I head into O'Keeley's. Would you like anything?"

"You have food?" For some reason, he seemed like an inept college kid.

"Yes."

She crossed her arms. "You go grocery shopping?"

"No. Rian gives me food. What's the point of having a brother who's a chef if you can't eat what he cooks?" He opened a container. "There's some lamb leftover."

"No, thank you."

"I'd like to come by the bar later if that's alright. I can bring you back afterward. I'm not too keen on you walking by yourself at night."

She steadied her breathing. He was considerate. Thoughtful. To everyone. Not just her. She knew why she reacted that way. After begging for her dad's attention and then trying to be what Hugo wanted her to be, Cathal seemed to take her as she was.

"I'd like that. Thanks." She went to her room and fixed her hair and at the last second, decided to leave it curly. It was a mass of hair when she didn't take the time to straighten it. Hugo didn't like it natural. And until he'd shown up at the bar, she still hadn't dropped that one habit, thinking it made her more attractive.

But she wasn't with Hugo, and she'd wear her hair whatever way she damn well pleased.

"Fiona—" Cathal stopped in the doorway, his eyes wide. "Your hair."

Until Cathal obviously hated it natural, too. Then she might reconsider—

"Good God, woman, you're going to be the death of me." He stalked across the room and kissed her. Not for anyone else or to put on a show.

He slipped his hands along the base of her neck and into her hair.

And she kissed him back, wondering, again, why she would even get her hopes up.

He stopped and stepped back, shock the only emotion registering.

"So—I usually straighten my hair." She pointed at it. It was stupid to feel exposed over leaving her hair natural. "Because my dad and Hugo hate it this way."

A shadow passed over his face, but he recovered with a sexy smile. She wanted to know what he really thought, not placate her, but he didn't seem inclined to reveal himself to her again.

"And I love it."

"I think you're just saying that."

He took a slow step closer, his voice deepening, his accent stronger. "I can show you again if you'd let me." He trailed a finger along the edge of her jaw, tipping her chin up and bringing their mouths close. "But I'm afraid that sleeping arrangement you wanted might not last."

Yes. She did want that.

"No. But thanks." She cleared her throat and stepped away. "For the demonstration."

Too many more of those moments and her resolve would be ancient history.

11

O'Keeley's wasn't busy, which suited Cathal at the moment. Brogan had texted him to come in and precisely what time since Selena would be gone. He passed the bar, gave Kami a quick, polite wave, and continued into the office without knocking.

Brogan stood in front of the unlit fireplace, a glass of whiskey in his hand.

Cathal's steps slowed. His brother rarely drank, let alone whiskey. "What's happened? The baby?"

His head shook slightly. "No. The baby is fine. Her due date is still in a couple weeks or so." He turned, crossing his arms. He looked shaken. "I have the video feed from the night the lawsuit claims that man was in our bar. Go look. It's on my computer."

Cathal sat down at the massive desk and started the video. Brogan crossed the room and stopped behind him.

"I was there?" Cathal watched the video a little longer. There was a larger crowd than usual, but still, nothing like he'd seen show up at Fiona's. O'Keeley's wasn't that type of bar. People usually waited for a table and had a drink.

They didn't even serve food at their bar like some restaurants.

Selena came into the scene, patting Cathal on the back. She mixed a margarita and passed it off.

"There." Brogan reached over his shoulder and pressed pause. "That's him."

Cathal zoomed in on the video. That was the man in question. It was the right date.

And Selena had served him.

He sat back, drumming his fingers on the desk. "Shit."

"Yes. It is."

"Did you tell her?"

"No." Brogan walked away. "I don't plan on telling her."

Cathal rose and leaned on the desk. "The video shows that the man isn't acting intoxicated."

"I don't want to show that video, Cathal. I can't have Selena implicated. What if they go after her personally?"

"Then we'll fight it," he snapped out.

Brogan finished the whiskey and set the glass down on the low table in front of the sofa. Surprisingly, the glass didn't break from the force.

"I want to take the fall. I'm going to tell the judge that I remember serving the guy."

"No." Cathal shook his head. "You aren't going to lie under oath. Not with a child on the way. You think Selena can't handle being the center of the lawsuit, do you really think she'd handle you being at the center any better?"

Brogan pointed at a letter on the desk. "They're asking for the video, if we have one, to identify who was serving that night. They want to call them to testify. Possibly hold them personally accountable."

Cathal ran a hand over his head as he read the letter. The answer was simple. "I'll take the blame."

"What?" Brogan sat down on the sofa like his legs gave out.

Crossing the room, Cathal stared at his brother. He leaned on the back of the chair that sat across from Brogan. "I'm behind the bar. I'll tell them that much."

"That will ruin you, Cathal. You know they'll drag out your past."

"What other option do we have? I have the least to lose of the three of us. Rian doesn't need the publicity. You and Selena don't need the stress. Hell, we all know that you keep this restaurant running."

"But your career?"

Cathal shrugged, trying to look easy-going. Relaxed. "I won't miss it."

Brogan rose, his chin kicked out and stubborn. "Try to find another way out of this. You're smart, although I don't say it nearly enough. Don't take the fall." He took a solid breath, his shoulders rising and then sagging. "Unless it's absolutely necessary."

Cathal dipped his chin in acknowledgment. He'd take care of his family, no matter the cost. They'd done the same for him.

Rian opened the office door, a bright smile in place with his arm around Mara's shoulders. "Good evening."

Shoving the letter from the lawyer to the side, Cathal held out his arms to hug Mara. "It is a good evening."

"Because you have your Fiona at your apartment now." Mara hugged him back. "I knew acting more yourself would work."

"That you did. And now she's well acquainted with my history." His brothers both looked at him. He didn't mind Fiona knowing. Not with how it'd ended up. "She's fine with it, it seems."

"Good." Brogan poured another whiskey. The man was stressed to the max. "That's good." He downed the glass in one swallow.

Cathal held out his hand as he crossed the room. "Go home to Selena. Rian and I can manage the place on a Wednesday night." He met Brogan's worried stare. "It will be fine."

Rian misunderstood the meaning of the statement. "Last word from Selena was that the doctor said the baby was in great health. Are you worried?"

"No. Not for the baby." Brogan reached for his suit jacket. "I think I will head home. Call me if anything arises." He left, his head cast down, his face looking defeated.

Cathal refused to let anything happen to Brogan or Selena. They wouldn't be brought into this fight. He'd make sure of it even if he lost his law license in the process. Even if he went back to jail.

Rian kissed Mara. "I'm going to check on the kitchen. Do you think you can help out on the floor if necessary?"

"Absolutely." Mara waited until Rian left before turning to Cathal. "So, how are things really with you and Fiona? It's not every day I have to venture into a bachelor's apartment and clean a bedroom out."

He grinned, feeling more himself as he suppressed the rest of the pain. "It was perfect. Thank you for doing that. She seemed to love it."

"I'm glad. When are you going to invite her here so we can get to know her better?"

"That's a tricky situation. I like Fiona. We've developed an odd type of friendship. And I'd like more time with her, but she's not in the mindset that we have an actual dating relationship." She still seemed shocked each time he kissed her. With the lawsuit pending, and him possibly about to take the fall for it, keeping her at a distance was the best option. She didn't need to be associated with him.

But he had a couple weeks at least to enjoy her company until she found a place to stay. It'd be impossible to have her in his apartment, see her every night and every morning, and not be able to kiss the woman.

That was like locking an alcoholic in a room full of the finest whiskey and telling him to refrain.

"I know," Mara began, startling Cathal out of his thoughts. "Invite her to go over the lesson on over-serving customers that you couldn't do Monday. Then she'd come here."

Would she help him? He'd only have to ask to find out. "I may see if she can. Can you ask Kami and Lindsay to come in tomorrow at eleven? I'll ask Jake and Chris later as well."

Mara smirked. "You don't want to ask Kami yourself?"

"No." She still made him uncomfortable. "I'll leave that up to you. I'll beg Fiona to come in tomorrow to do that before she goes and opens her bar. Might even persuade her to eat lunch with me while she's here."

"Good." She started to walk from the room but stopped at the door. "Cathal?"

He raised his eyebrows. "Yes?"

"Rian told me about your past. No woman that really knows you would walk away because of it."

Cathal nodded and agreed to some extent that Fiona wouldn't run because of what happened before he left Ireland. She'd even moved in with him, and she'd seen the anger first-hand. That wasn't his worry.

All the gut-wrenching feelings came from knowing that, eventually, he'd end up hurting her. Not physically. He'd never in his life lay a hand on a woman. But, when it happened again when he couldn't control himself when something set him off, and he turned into the "Hulk," as Selena called him, that's when he'd hurt Fiona.

Simply being associated with him would hurt her.

And now, with Brogan's request, his offer, on his mind, he'd have to walk away before the trial.

He left the office, determined to keep himself busy until closing. To get his mind back where it should be. Before Fiona. When he could compartmentalize his emotions.

DAMN, but Cathal drove her crazy. She'd left his apartment still reeling from the result of having slept in his arms during their nap. She understood him better. His past. Why he acted the way he did.

But now, she watched him serve a customer a beer, smiling and acting the way he always did. To have him switch back to the big flirt annoyed the hell out of her.

He'd glided right into her bar, stepped behind the counter, and took the next customer's order. They were overly busy, so she appreciated the help. But his magnetic personality and gift of conversation lured every female in a five-block radius.

And the four college-aged girls at the end of the bar had nearly monopolized his time.

She rolled her eyes as they giggled about something he'd said.

Their living arrangements, kisses, didn't mean they were an item. They weren't exclusive. But she would not sleep in his apartment if he had a woman in there. She'd rather sleep in her bar.

And that was saying something.

Cathal strode across the wooden floor toward her. His

practiced smile in place. But it wasn't real. She could almost differentiate between the two now.

"Have your groupies run you off?" She continued drying the pint glass before setting it into the cooler to chill. "Since you gave me a key, I can take myself back to the apartment so you can go do whatever it is you do with them." Just suggesting it put a strange pain in her stomach. She ignored it.

He grinned wider. "I'd rather sleep alone knowing you were a few walls away than have the company."

"I don't believe that."

"You're right." He stepped to her, slipping his hand along her waist until he reached her lower back. He pulled her tight against his body. "I'd rather sleep with you, but if it's not you, then I'll be alone."

He kissed her. A sensual, drawn-out kiss that ended with a few of her regular customers clapping. Cathal rested his forehead against hers.

He kept his voice low and didn't release her. "Don't ever question my want of you, Fiona. It pains me. It hits so deep."

The irritation with him from before left her body, and she relaxed against him. "It's probably stupid to be jealous in a fake relationship anyway."

He hooked his finger under her chin, tilting it up until she met his eyes. They were a deep, dark blue. "Real or fake, if I'm with you, you have no reason to be jealous." He brushed his lips over hers and pulled away.

Pretending as though her knees felt steadier than they were, she turned back to the customers waiting for a drink.

They worked in tandem until closing, Cathal still joking and cutting up with everyone that came up to place their order with him. She tried to reconcile that the flirt, the fun-loving man, was still the same guy who wrestled with demons every day.

Cathal held the door open to his apartment, letting her pass through first. "I have a favor to ask of you," he began, tossing his keys into a bowl on the counter.

She set her purse down on a chair. "What is it?"

"Can you come to O'Keeley's tomorrow at eleven? I have the bartenders coming in to go over that training they all took. Brogan wants a follow-up to it."

She trailed behind him into the living room and sat on the sofa beside him. It was nearly two-thirty in the morning, and she'd fall asleep soon. Possibly sitting upright on his sofa if he kept her too long. "What do you want me to do?"

"Go over it with them."

"Me? Why don't you do it?" She yawned and covered her mouth, setting her head on the back of the sofa.

"I tried. They don't pay attention to me."

She laughed. "The women probably pay you too much attention."

He rubbed a finger over his lip. "Something like that. It could be the last time I tried, I wasn't in the mood and it didn't go as planned. I threatened to have Brogan do it, but with Selena so close to her due date, he's a bit of a nutcase."

Fiona yawned again. "Sorry. Then I'll do it. No problem. Wait-" she lifted her head "-I have lunch planned with my parents tomorrow."

"Where?" He held out his hands. "Bring them to O'Keeley's."

"You really want to meet my dad again at your restaurant? What if he has an outburst?"

Cathal leaned forward, giving her a sweet, soft kiss. "Believe me. It won't be the first time O'Keeley's has been disturbed by an unruly patron. Eleven?"

She nodded and stood up. "Eleven it is. Goodnight, Cathal."

"Goodnight, Fiona."

She left him on the sofa, walking to her room and lightly shutting the door. Tomorrow should be interesting.

12

"Good morning," Kami said as she walked behind the bar. She skimmed her finger along the counter, her dark eyes locked on him. He didn't need this.

Cathal pulled another clean glass from the washer and set it in the cooler. "Good morning." He kept his head down, working, wishing she'd walk away. No such luck. The woman was determined to grab his attention, but instead, she simply made him uncomfortable.

She stopped less than a foot from him, leaning her hip on the bar. "Are you going to be here all day? I'd hate it if I didn't get to see you later tonight."

He shifted away, checking the level of the ice in the bin and basically doing nothing of any importance. The woman had him cornered. He suddenly held sympathy for animals lashing out when trapped. He slowly took two steps to the other side of the bar.

She shifted, blocking that exit as well.

He crossed his arms, facing her and addressing the issue. "I hope I haven't sent mixed signals, Kami, but I'm not interested in starting anything with you."

"Is the no dating policy the only reason?" She took a slow step. "Because we can always keep it between the two of us."

He'd typically say something funny to a woman when he wasn't interested. Make a joke, flirt a little, let them down easy, and move on. But now, he felt a small shred of panic. Mostly that because of his reputation, no one would believe the truth.

She set her hand on the counter.

He backed up against the bar, gripping the dishrag in his hand. The chemicals of her perfume choked him.

"I can come back if you're busy."

Cathal snapped around. "Fiona!"

Fiona crossed her arms, her irritation evident. "That's me. It looks like you might have forgotten my name for a moment."

No. More like she saved him from an extremely uncomfortable situation. But the smirk on Kami's face bothered him. She really didn't get it. He wasn't interested. He couldn't picture himself with anyone *except* Fiona.

"Let me introduce you to Kami. She's the bartender that hit on your date last week."

Kami's lips pressed into a tight line as she looked away.

Fiona's eyes shifted, taking in Kami and judging the situation. She couldn't really think he'd hit on Kami.

"Kami, this is my girlfriend, Fiona."

With the use of her title, that he didn't consider fake any longer, the strain around Fiona's eyes eased. Good. Fiona didn't have to worry about competition from Kami or any other woman.

"Girlfriend?" Kami laughed. "You? I don't believe it."

Cathal squeezed between Kami and the bar, stepping sideways until he was finally free. "Yes. She is." He walked to the end of the bar and then around to greet Fiona. He loved the little gasp he always felt when he kissed her without warning. So, he did.

His hands cupped her cheeks before sliding into her mass of red hair. She'd left it down and a little wild. Her hands gripped his wrists, her lips willing to match his kiss.

"What exactly are you teaching the bartenders, Cathal?" Rian asked from behind him.

Cathal ended the kiss. Fiona's eyes were bright, and a small smile hovered on her lips. "Hi."

"Hi," she murmured before shoving him away. "We have an audience, and you have company."

Cathal flicked his hand in the air. "That's my brother. Not company."

Fiona stepped around Cathal. "Hi, I'm Fiona." She shook Rian's hand. "I already met Brogan."

"Yes, you did." Cathal set his hands on her shoulders, tugging her back against his chest. He loved the physical connection with her. "This one is the chef. Most of the time, he's moody and generally unpleasant to be around, but he cooks fairly decent, so we allow him to stay. Are you here to help with the bartender review?"

"No. I came because Mara is setting up for a spontaneous baby shower for Selena. She and Katie have it in their mind to host one tonight." Rian rolled his shoulders. "Too much pink in the condo."

Fiona relaxed back against Cathal. "Do you not like pink?"

Cathal laughed. "Rian hates color."

"I don't hate color. Mara has put several colorful things in our condo."

"I think you have one new pillow on your sofa and a festive rug in the kitchen."

"Exactly." Rian dismissed Cathal and focused back on Fiona. "By the way, what are you doing this evening, Fiona? Would you like to go to the baby shower?"

"I have to work."

Cathal leaned down, giving her shoulders a squeeze. "I can cover for you if you want to go."

"You'd do that?" She shifted, looking up at him with disbelief.

Why was it so hard for her to trust that she could rely on him? It looked to shock her each time he stepped in to help. Granted, he was on new ground with her or any woman. He enjoyed the feeling of being committed to Fiona. And, for the time being, he'd do so without worry of the future. The pain of losing her would come eventually.

"Of course," he said. "I know Selena would enjoy your company, and you need a night off." He kissed her. "Go. Have fun."

The door opened; three more bartenders walked into the restaurant.

"I think your group is all here." Rian smiled down at Fiona. "Cathal said your parents would be here today. I'll make their lunch, so just send Cathal or Katie in with your order."

"Wow. Okay." She blinked, looking like a cute surprised owl as Rian disappeared back into the kitchen. "You don't have to do all this for me."

"Why not?" He'd figured she'd like to know Rian made her parents' meals.

"I mean, we're not—" She trailed off and glanced around.

"I'm not going to wait for you to finish that statement. While you're living with me and you'll let me keep kissing you, then we're together. The. End." He kissed the tip of her nose. "Now, let's see if my bartenders will listen to you better than they would me."

"You're just too pretty. It's distracting." She patted his cheek and stepped away.

"Me? You're gorgeous, so I don't see the difference."

She cut her eyes at him over her shoulder. "I'm meaner." She walked up to the edge of the bar. The six bartenders who'd shown up sat at the tables in front of the bar. "Hi. I'm Fiona Grant. Cathal asked me to go over the course you all took online about over-serving individuals."

Kami raised her hand but didn't wait on Fiona to call on her. "Question. Why are you teaching us and not Cathal? Are you with the state or something?"

"No. I own a bar, and I've taken the same course as you. They just wanted to go over some of the highlights from the course. Now, what are some of the effects of alcohol on a customer?"

Kami and the woman beside her started whispering. It was the same thing they'd done to Cathal, although his patience had run a little thin that day to handle it.

"You. You feel the need to talk while I'm doing this so you can be the one to answer it." Fiona crossed her arms, staring down Kami.

Kami shifted, not looking the least bit worried about Fiona's sharp tone. She wiggled her fingers in his direction.

He tried for a serious expression. Something stern that Brogan would use.

Fiona cleared her throat. "Any time now."

Kami rolled her eyes and crossed her legs. "Alcohol makes people drunk. What else is there to know?"

"If your customer takes six shots in less than thirty minutes, and then gets up from his seat and leaves, do you think he's sober enough to drive home?"

She gave Fiona a bland expression. "Of course not. But how do I tell someone they can't drive themselves home. They're grown adults. They should be responsible for knowing when they've had enough to drink. I'm not a babysitter."

Fiona's voice tightened. "You don't serve them the six shots without casually asking them exactly that question. You're bartenders, which means you should know how to carry on a conversation. Be friendly. Be flirty. Act, however you want to act, to get the answer you need to make sure the people you serve stay safe, *and* they don't injure anyone else."

Fiona continued to pepper the bartenders with questions for the next thirty minutes. Kami eventually gave up on her campaign to get Cathal in trouble, with both Brogan and Fiona, and she finally focused on the lesson.

The meeting ended as Fiona's parents walked into O'Keeley's. Cathal wasn't nervous about the meeting. He expected the cold shoulder from Mr. Grant. Maybe a few tense words. But he'd hoped to find himself on Mrs. Grant's good side.

Fiona favored her mother. Her nose and cheeks were the same shapes. She had strawberry blond hair, nothing like Fiona's vibrant red, but they both shared similar smooth, ivory skin.

"Are you ready?" Fiona's voice held a touch of anxiety.

Her father scowled at Cathal.

"Sure, darling." Cathal smiled and interlaced his fingers with hers. "I'm looking forward to this."

"Liar."

His smile widened. "And hopefully, you'll be the only one to notice that."

She squeezed his hand, and they crossed the dining

room. He took the lead. He'd try to make the lunch as comfortable for her as possible, even if it meant deflecting all the conflict toward himself.

Mrs. Grant held her arms open. Fiona gave her a hug, tentatively dropping his hand to do so. He missed the connection immediately but turned and held his hand out to her da.

"Nice to see you again." Cathal's hand hovered in the air. At the last moment, Mr. Grant shook his hand and grunted.

"And you're Cathal. I just love your restaurant. It's charming." Mrs. Grant gave him a hug. Her silk blouse slid underneath his hand as he touched her back. "Nice to meet you."

"Nice to meet you, too." Cathal snagged Fiona's hand again. "I see where Fiona gets her beauty."

Mrs. Grant's cheeks turned pink.

Mr. Grant grunted again.

"Katie will be our waitress." He caught Katie's eye and motioned her over. "And Rian came in today to cook your lunch."

Mrs. Grant looked at Fiona for an explanation. "Who?"

Fiona leaned into Cathal. "Cathal's brother, Rian O'Keeley. He's the chef."

"That's the chef that Mary Ann and Ginger told me about." Mrs. Grant touched Fiona's shoulder. "I think Mary Ann may have a crush on him. She met him at a special event here about a year ago."

Mr. Grant's chin dipped. "I've heard of him." His eyes skipped to Cathal. "I didn't realize that was your brother."

Great. Rian's fame made the man look halfway friendly at Cathal. Maybe not half. A quarter. But since his earlier expression was complete contempt, Cathal would use his leverage with Rian and take a quarter.

"If you'd like, I can see if he'll make something different from the menu. He likes having challenges like that."

Katie raised her eyebrows, looking like she tried not to laugh out loud. She knew Rian and knew he'd pitch a major fit being put on the spot. But Cathal had helped Rian along with Mara. He could return the favor.

Mr. Grant rolled his shoulders. The man wasn't tall, maybe five-eight. The same height as Fiona. Even with a receding hairline and stomach soft, Mr. Grant still managed to intimidate Cathal.

Even if Fiona claimed her da didn't have any hold over her, no man wanted the woman's da to hate him.

"That would be interesting, I suppose," Mr. Grant finally said.

Cathal set his arm across Fiona's shoulders. "Then, I'll let Katie get you settled with drinks." He kissed Fiona's temple. "I'll be right back."

He walked across the restaurant, past the bar where thankfully Kami didn't say anything to him, and into the kitchen.

Rian worked alongside another cook, showing him how to plate a dish. He glanced up as Cathal entered.

"Ah, are they here? What did they order?"

"Nothing. I told them you'd fix something spectacular. You know, one of those award-winning dishes I'm always reading about. Now is the time, brother."

Rian paused. He straightened, his eyes narrowing at Cathal. "You told them I'd fix them *something*. Any idea what they'd like?" He held his arms out. "It'd be nice to have some direction with what I have to work with. And award-winning dishes don't pop out of thin air."

"Damn drama queen. Give me two options, and I'll let you know." Cathal crossed his arms. "You asked me once not to screw things up with Mara; I'd ask you to have the same consideration now."

The fight left Rian, and his shoulders relaxed. "You're right. Let me rummage through the kitchen and think about it. I'll come out and speak with them myself."

Cathal nodded. "Thanks. Her da has heard of you. It seemed to lessen the hate in his eyes."

"You really like her, don't you?"

He shoved his hands in his pockets, considering his answer. What it meant. "I do. I don't know how to handle the future of it, but we're fine for the moment, I think. She enjoys herself with me, and for once, I can be myself."

Rian didn't smile or joke. He knew exactly how hard it was to let his guard down. "It's nice, isn't it? Being yourself for the first time in a long time."

"You were yourself with Brogan and me. Or did we only see the sunny side of your personality?"

Rian's grin was quick. "You know what I mean. And Mara's a tad bit prettier company to relax around than either you or Brog."

"I agree completely." Cathal left the kitchen, walking across the dining room, enjoying the way Fiona watched him. He had no business in a relationship. His mind was programmed to take care of a woman, protect her, care for her. In another life, one without the dark cloud hanging over his, he'd have been proud to have a wife like Fiona.

Too bad he couldn't very well provide for a woman from prison, and he didn't trust himself not to end up back there again.

Case in point was the lawsuit against O'Keeley's. He'd take the fall in a heartbeat for Selena. His sister-in-law's name would remain out of the courtroom if he oversaw the case. Not only did he know he'd protect her because she was family, but Brogan deserved it. Because if Cathal didn't take the fall, then his brother would.

A line creased Fiona's forehead when he sat down. Her hand immediately landed on his thigh. Comfort. The woman read him easier than anyone he'd ever met.

He squeezed her hand. "Rian said he'd come out here with a few options, let you pick what you'd like after he took stock in the kitchen."

Mrs. Grant's eyes lit up. "I can't wait to tell the women at the country club. They won't believe it. I read an article he did a few months ago about a fusion between Southern cuisine and Irish, and it sounds heavenly." She patted Mr. Grant's forearm. "Don't you remember me telling you about that?"

"Yes." Mr. Grant's eyes locked onto Cathal. "You own this restaurant, *and* you're a lawyer."

"That's right. But, I'll admit, other than handling the law side of O'Keeley's, my brothers are the ones who make it run as it does. I help when needed, but that's about all."

Fiona leaned forward. "Cathal has been helping at my bar lately."

"Yes. I saw how he helped the other day." Mr. Grant watched his daughter for a long moment. "I still think this is a mistake."

"I know you do." Fiona's nose tilted up.

"You're ruining decades of planning."

"I know that, too. But you can't use my life to run your business. If you want to pass everything to Hugo, go right ahead. I won't fight it. I enjoy what I'm doing now."

Mr. Grant's jaw bunched. His face became a ruddy shade of red. And he turned his glare to Cathal. "If you knew what was best for Fiona, you'd convince her to come back to the life we planned for her instead of keeping her here with you."

"I'd assumed that you'd want her to be happy." He brought the back of her hand to his lips, his eyes locked with her da. "As long as I make your daughter happy, I'll be here with her. The minute she's unhappy, she's free to go."

He pushed away from the sinking feeling that he'd make her unhappy in the end. Either he'd walk away, or she'd sink with him.

But, for the moment, he'd be everything she needed.

13

Fiona assumed she'd like Selena and Mara. Rian's apartment sat near the top of a ritzy building. Nothing like where Cathal lived. Cathal's apartment was more average. A regular looking place in an ordinary-looking complex. Rian's had a doorman, valet parking, and marble floors with granite countertops.

Mara wore a soft pink dress with small straps and stood barefoot in the living room. She turned as Fiona stepped into the condo. Smiling wide, she motioned Fiona forward. "Yay! Rian said you might show up. Come in and close the door. I think you complete our small party."

Fiona scanned the room. Pink balloons were tied to elegant bar stools. A banner with "Rosie" in large pink letters hung over a stone fireplace. Three platters of various pink desserts sat out along the glass coffee table. Underneath the pink, she could see what Cathal meant. Rian had a black-and-white theme in his apartment.

Selena pushed off the sofa, her stomach almost as wide as she was tall. Her white shirt, maybe a men's shirt, was stretched over her baby bump, and black yoga pants hugged her slight curves. "Welcome to my surprise baby shower! Nice to meet you again." Her honey-colored eyes sparkled with excitement. Her dark blond hair hung loosely around her shoulders. She pointed at the bag in Fiona's hand. "You did not have to bring a gift. This is an excuse to sit with girlfriends without Brogan hovering over me, ready to catch Rosie should she make an early appearance."

"And to eat cake." Katie came in from the kitchen, holding out a glass of what looked like pink champagne. The tips of her stark, white hair were dyed fuchsia. "Don't get your hopes up; it's non-alcoholic."

"It looks delicious. I'm glad to be invited. It's been a while since I've done something other than work in my bar." Like nearly a year. She liked it that way, staying busy, working hard. She proved to herself she could do it. She didn't need her degree or her parents' money. In fact, Fiona had to do something with the twenty-thousand dollars sitting in a little checking account they'd set up for her. Write them back a check, maybe. They probably wouldn't take it.

"I understand. Sometimes, it feels as though we live at O'Keeley's. Well, before I got to this point. Now, I have to make sure Brogan is sleeping *hard* and try and sneak out of the house." She smirked and sipped the pink drink. "He doesn't seem to mind the extra forty pounds and gut."

"It's not a gut," Mara said as she sat down on the sofa. "You have a baby in there."

"And soon, when the sweet little thing is in my arms, it will no longer be considered a baby bump. No. At that point, it will be a gut!" Selena held her hands up. "I'm completely prepared for that."

Katie nudged Fiona. "And if you ever saw the way Brogan looks at Selena, he won't care what your body looks like after you have a baby. You could turn into that monster from *Aliens,* and the man would be hot on your tail."

Selena wrinkled her nose. "Funny you say that since it feels like the monster from *Aliens* is currently living inside me. I swear this child is going to come out with six elbows, three knees, and no head. I can't find the head to save my life. She sticks her butt out sometimes." She rubbed her stomach, a small line forming along her forehead. "At least I think it's a butt. Maybe she has two of those instead of a head?"

The women laughed, and Fiona settled in on the sofa across from Selena. These women were real. Nice. They made her feel welcome—and miss having friends.

After a few more laughs and eating pink cupcakes, cake pops, and some type of chocolate ganache covered in pink chocolate, Fiona passed Selena the gift she'd brought.

"I wanted to get it monogrammed but wasn't sure of her initials. If that's something you'd like, I'll take it with me and have it done." Fiona waited as Selena pulled out a yellow, hooded towel covered in tiny roses and a set of pink washcloths. "It's such a soft towel; I wandered around the store, hoping to find one in my size."

Selena rubbed it along her cheek. "I may have to borrow this from my daughter at some point. I'd love her name on it."

"Alright. I'll have it done and send it back to you through Cathal."

At the mention of Cathal's name, Selena's eyes narrowed. "About Cathal. I've been trying to find a way to ask you how's it going?"

Katie groaned and sat back. "Just torture me."

"Please, you've moved on," Selena said. "I met Vivian. She's perfect for you."

Mara finished her drink and sat forward, sitting the glass on the coffee table. "I'm curious as well. I saw the state of that apartment before I decorated your room. Has it reverted back?"

"No. But I do notice him setting something down and walking away before turning back and picking it up. I'm not a neat freak or anything, so it doesn't bother me." She grimaced. "I'll probably go through and give everything a deep cleaning, though."

"I don't think he'd complain if you did." Selena rested a hand on her stomach. "No matter what the circumstances, I'm glad you're there with him." She and Mara shared a glance.

They both had to know about Cathal's past. His anger issues. She couldn't imagine having someone in her family be in such mental pain and not be able to do anything about it. Or maybe they didn't see it that way. Fiona saw the sadness underneath what he gave to the rest of the world. And she wanted to take it away.

But he wouldn't let her.

Katie held out her gift to Selena. "Here. I'm next."

Selena pulled out a baby onesie that had *Rosie the Riveter* on the front. "Thank you! I may have to dress her up like this for her first Halloween."

Reality pushed Fiona back into the sofa. Would she be around to see that? She hoped so. Even if Cathal always reminded her that he didn't consider their relationship fake, he'd not fully committed either. He let her see his pain, told her his story, and then pulled away. And she wanted to help.

The man was hard-headed and stubborn and determined to suffer alone.

But he didn't have to.

"Are you alright?" Mara asked in a low whisper. Katie

and Selena were on the other sofa, still laughing together. She shifted a little closer. "You look upset."

"I'm fine." Fiona glanced at her watch. "I do need to get going, though. Even if Cathal told me he'd handle the bar for the rest of the night, I know it has to be getting pretty full in there."

"What about help? It seems like you could hire someone to help out."

"I couldn't hire anyone at first because I didn't have the money. Then, it became a point of doing it on my own. But, now, after having help when Cathal is there, I might finally hire another bartender."

Mara patted Fiona's leg. "I think you should hire Cathal."

That statement made Selena sit up straight. "Hire Cathal? But he already works two jobs."

Mara chewed on her bottom lip for a moment, suddenly seeming unsure. "I know, but he's seemed happier lately. I wonder if the change of scenery, away from his brothers and us, hasn't helped just as much as being with Fiona."

"Happier?" Katie threw her head back and laughed. "I assume that man sleeps with a smile on his face."

The three women shared a look but didn't respond. That wasn't the real Cathal. Selena and Mara apparently knew that, but Fiona thought maybe they didn't know it all. Cathal hid something else. It was like he was a maze. He showed the world the outside of the maze, and that was like a seductive, fun carnival.

The next layer he'd let Fiona and his family in to see. The smile disappeared, and the rides stopped. It was like Cathal could finally be still.

But there was another part, an inner section that Cathal kept closed to everyone. That scared her. Not that he'd keep something from her. She didn't exactly want to get into the emotions involved with Hugo. Everyone kept a little bit of themselves locked away.

With Cathal, it was different. He honestly thought his soul was dark, and it made Fiona wonder precisely how dark he kept that innermost chamber of his mind. It scared her.

Mostly because she didn't know how to help.

And she was afraid she couldn't.

CATHAL'S brief conversation with Brogan before he went to Fiona's bar, played over and over in his mind. He served her customers automatically, making conversation without paying attention. Giving out change. Running credit cards. But Brogan had asked him if he'd found a way out of having to try and take the fall for Selena.

And he hadn't.

But he hadn't focused and worked hard on finding an answer yet. He'd put the time in later.

Because the girl of his dreams just arrived. Carrying a dozen pink balloons.

"Those are interesting party favors." He bumped one of Fiona's balloons with his finger.

Fiona tied them to Cathal's "old" chair at the end of the bar. He'd not sat there for a while now, always opting to get behind the bar and help.

"I just want to make sure your seat is festive should you ever want to sit there again."

"I'll be sure to keep my butt next to you and work." He kissed her and then smiled. "You taste like sweets and dessert."

She set a hand over her stomach. "That's because I ate so many treats that I feel as big as Selena now."

In one brief, unexpected flash, he thought of what it'd be like to have a child with Fiona. God, if being with a woman, feeling responsible, gave him a sinking feeling, adding a child into the mix would make Cathal go insane. Who'd want a da who'd gone to prison and could end up back there?

Or who had their law license revoked for over-serving at a bar when found guilty? Because that was the easiest way out. Show up in the courtroom in a couple weeks and tell the judge it was his fault. Shoulder all the responsibility. That didn't scare him.

Possibly going to prison or losing his job didn't scare him.

Knowing that once he did, he would lose Fiona. He'd never feel her kiss, watch her, or touch her again. Because even if she claimed that his past didn't bother her, it had to. Especially when it all came front and center again, and she was guilty by association.

Her cool hand touched his cheek. "Come back," she murmured and then brushed her lips lightly across his. "Cathal?"

He held onto her hips, wanting to tug her close but refraining. "I'm here."

"No. You're not. Why don't you head out? The crowd isn't heavy."

"But walking you home..."

"I'll be fine."

"No." He shook his head, getting out of his emotions and various scenarios that might happen. "I need to do some work, but I'll come back and pick you up."

After another kiss that was too brief, she nodded. "Alright. I'm closing on time, so be here at two-fifteen."

"Got it." He left, without another kiss, without a damn plan as to how to break things off with her. But first, he'd try to find the best way to handle the case against O'Keeley's. He'd find out what they were responsible for, come up with a fair settlement, all without sinking the restaurant or his family.

It still seemed impossible that the drunk driver was intoxicated when he left O'Keeley's, and they would have known at the time, putting them liable. It was never a question they'd help the injured man if possible. All the brothers had agreed to that, even if they hadn't laid out the specifics.

But before they could go that route, he needed a plan. He'd promised Brogan that he'd work his hardest on the case, and that's one thing he didn't do, break his promises.

14

A faint light shone underneath Fiona's door. She didn't know what woke her up, but typically, Cathal kept his apartment in complete darkness at night, so the light was odd. She adjusted her nightshirt and flannel pants and walked to the door, cracking it open.

Cathal sat on the sofa, papers spread out across the coffee table. With head in his hand, his elbow was propped on his knee. He didn't wear a shirt, and the muscles in his back looked tight and tense.

"Hey," Fiona said, pulling the door open and stepping out.

He swiveled his head around. "What are you doing up?"

She crossed her arms over her body, feeling unusually vulnerable with him. They'd kissed already. Why did it feel as though the intimacy of standing there, in his living room at four in the morning, was new? She'd lived with her fiancé for two years and never once had this rush of nerves.

"I'm not sure why I woke up, but I saw the light under the door, and thought I'd make sure everything was alright."

She scanned his face. His eyes were tired. No. Tired didn't describe what she saw.

Pure exhaustion.

"Why are you up?"

He motioned to the paper. "This was playing over in my mind."

"Is it the divorce case?" He'd had a hard time processing the abuse. With his meeting tomorrow, maybe he was making some last-minute preparations.

He shook his head. "No. This is the lawsuit against O'Keeley's. I keep going in circles."

"It's the middle of the night. There's no way you can even think straight at this point. Maybe you should try to get some sleep and then look at it again in the morning."

He leaned forward and lifted several sheets of paper and appeared to start reading again. "I'm fine. I don't sleep much anyway."

"If you'd have said that to me last month, I'd have told you maybe you shouldn't be out with a woman every night."

He smirked. "You'd have probably been correct."

"But as far as I know, you've been completely faithful to our pretend relationship."

He cut his eyes at her.

"You know what I mean."

He grunted and looked back at the paper he held. "I don't always like to sleep, Fiona. The women, the whiskey, it helps me sleep in oblivion. Not with the memories."

Her arms dropped to her side. He'd unlocked one more small piece of the maze, letting her in. And it was as dark as she'd imagined. She wanted to hold him and tell him it was alright, but it wasn't. Not for him.

"Cathal-"

"No. I don't need your sympathy. I need to focus on this lawsuit. It's a good thing that I can't sleep. Gives me more time to work on this." He set a piece of paper to the side and picked up another one. "Go back to bed."

Tough guy. He had as much pride as she did. And he was suffering for it. How long had he been like this? Months? Years? Surely, he hadn't been like this for nearly fifteen years, suffering alone.

"You really need to get some sleep."

"Why?" He snapped out the question. "I've functioned just fine the way I am without you being here at four a.m. to mother me."

She didn't take the bait to fight with him. She waited until he looked up from his paper. "Because you look like you've been run over by a truck."

"If you're looking for a compliment in return, I'm not in the mood at the moment."

She couldn't just leave him on the sofa and go back to bed. Caring for the man was making it hard to keep her distance. And he made it so damn easy to care for. He supported everyone around him, although they didn't see it like that. But she saw it.

She saw him.

His raw emotions and pain tore at her heart.

Right then, she knew what Cathal needed. He thrived on physical touch. It centered him. Calmed the chaos in his mind. She wouldn't have sex with him as a sleep aid, but she'd try to relax him.

"Come to bed, Cathal."

"I said-" His head shot up.

She smiled. "You heard me." She turned and walked into her room. As she expected, the lamp in the living room turned off, and he followed her. This would not end in sex. That was a promise to herself.

"Lie down."

Cathal's eyes were open and awake now. "I didn't realize you were so bossy in the bedroom. I'm game as long as you promise I get a turn next."

She gave his shoulder a light shove. His skin felt hot. Did he have a fever, or was he usually that warm?

"We aren't doing anything kinky. Lie down on your stomach."

"Damn shame." He crawled into her bed. He wore nothing but a pair of gym shorts and those rested at the top of his perfect butt. She'd have to admire it later. For now, she'd try to get him to fall asleep.

Taking a breath, needing the courage, she climbed onto the bed and sat straddling his lower back.

"I think you have me facing the wrong direction, love," Cathal mumbled, his face partially covered with a pillow.

"No." She held her hands out, hesitating, before resting them on his shoulders. She pressed down on the tight, tense muscles.

He groaned.

That made her smile. She worked on his shoulders, back, arms for nearly twenty minutes. His deep breaths signaled that he'd finally fallen asleep. It must be horrible for him. No wonder she'd seen him nap several times. Did his brothers know he couldn't sleep? Had he talked to a doctor?

She slid off him, trying not to wake him, before lying down on the pillow beside him.

His arm reached out for her, pulling her back against his chest as he shifted. Lips pressed against her neck.

"Remember what I said about choosing between a massage and sex."

"If you got to pick between the two, you'd pick sex." She reached back and patted his thigh. "You didn't have a choice. I thought you'd gone to sleep."

"I had. But the scent of you, that sweet honeysuckle smell, woke me up." He tugged on her hip, rolling her to her back. "Face me." The quiet, unusually dominant demand made her toes curl. He continued to pull her until he held her the way he wanted. "Better," he whispered before his lips returned to her throat.

His hand slipped underneath her knee, anchoring her leg to his hip.

"Cathal..."

"I know. Just enjoy yourself for a little bit." She felt his lips smile against her collarbone. "For you, that means don't think."

"But that's when trouble happens."

"No. I won't let it. No matter how much you beg for me in a few minutes."

She snorted. Not the sexiest sound in the world when a gorgeous man with a killer accent did wicked things with his lips to her neck. She managed to make the ultimate promise.

"I will not beg."

CHALLENGES WERE FUN. In most instances. If his only test was to make sure Fiona felt unbelievable in his arms, then rising to that challenge would be an easy feat. But he'd promised her no sex, and, at that moment, he didn't know how he'd survive.

Her body was made for him: every single inch, every moan, built-up pressure. Her skin softer than silk pushed him right to the edge. Her breathing, a little uneven, matched his own. All the fun things he'd wanted to do to her, with her, flicked through his mind like a video on fast forward. His eyes squeezed tight, his hand nearly bruising her skin.

She was an obsession. A drug. The more he touched, kissed, the more he wanted. Craved.

When he finally held her breasts in his hands, it confirmed that he'd found Heaven. The size, the weight, the taste sent him into a frenzy of ideas.

But he'd promised her.

That meant he wouldn't rip the thin shirt from her body. A fact he repeated in his mind until his thoughts finally evened out, and he gained control again. With every other woman, he waited for them to make a move. Analyzed their actions. Tried to figure out what they wanted. Needed. Liked. Nothing but a well-rehearsed dance.

Until Fiona. Everything he'd ever experienced with another woman paled in comparison.

The pounding in his blood shook him hard.

Her hands didn't help his restraint. They'd roamed all over his body, greedy little things that tortured him with each touch. Her nails running along his spine. Her fingers digging into his shoulders.

Her teeth skimmed along the edge of his ear. "You were right. I'm on the verge of begging. You are killing me," she whispered, arching closer to him.

"Good. I'm not alone in the slaughter." He forced his hand from her breast and down her stomach. "How far can I take this?"

"Please," she panted before covering his lips with a kiss.

Any other time, he'd have laughed at the polite request, but at the moment, he had a redhead in his arms who, as soon as he settled his hand between her legs, came apart.

The arm she'd wrapped around his shoulder tightened as a sharp, breathy gasp escaped. She buried her head against his neck, his name a whisper from her lips.

It was the sexiest damn thing that had ever happened between him and a woman.

Because it was Fiona.

Her body began to relax. He pulled down her T-shirt before he ignored reason and stripped her naked. He kissed her lips and felt the slight tremble. Was it him or her?

"Cathal-"

He kissed her again, harder. He didn't want whatever she had to say. They needed to leave what happened between them in the dark. Words would mess it up. Analyzing it would make tomorrow uncomfortable.

"Go to sleep, Fiona."

She moved closer to him, settling her head on his shoulder, her arm draped across his waist, their legs intertwined. He stared at the ceiling, barely seeing the outline of the ceiling fan. Finding Fiona, realizing too late she was perfect for him, screwed up everything. His fingers trailed up and down her spine.

He never wanted to find that *one* person that made him want to give up everything. If she stayed much longer, he'd start to think it could work. And that made him selfish. She deserved someone who was in control of their life, their emotions.

He couldn't even sleep without the nightmares waking him. That wasn't the type of life she was meant to live. He'd seen her parents. Smelled their wealth. Watched Fiona shift from the sassy bartender into a class above him. He'd take that away from her if he kept her to himself.

Her hand began to stroke his chest. "Go to sleep, Cathal."

He pressed his lips to the top of her head, breathing in the honeysuckle scent and finally closing his eyes.

15

The softness of Fiona pressed against him brought Cathal fully awake from a deep sleep. He blinked in the sunlight before glancing at his watch. Eight-thirty.

He had mediation in thirty minutes. "Darling, I need to get up." His entire body felt relaxed. He could stay in bed with her all morning if that were an option. Calling in sick sounded like a damn good option until he thought of Mrs. Cabot. She needed him there to settle the divorce.

Fiona stretched alongside his body like a cat. He'd noticed her doing that when they'd taken a nap together her first day there. Her hair was tangled on the pillow, and her blue eyes bright when she opened them. She was beautiful.

"I have to be at the office in thirty minutes."

She sat up. "Oh. Then you need to get going."

"Probably." He ran a hand down her back. "I'd rather stay here with you."

Her eyes pinched at the corners. "Did you sleep?"

"I did, actually." He pushed up and slid over to sit beside her. "Thank you."

"No bad dreams?"

"None." He pushed the tangled length of her hair over her shoulder. "Impossible to have a bad dream with you beside me."

She huffed.

He cut her off before she could argue. He kissed her cheek. "I didn't say they weren't dirty dreams."

She half-laughed. "At least you're honest." She gave him a soft shove off the bed. "Go. Don't be late."

Walking away from her warmth almost killed him. He'd not slept, all night, next to a woman in a long time. If she'd invite him back, he'd gladly spend the rest of their time together curled around her.

After a quick shower and shave and dressed in a suit, he walked back through the living room. Still wearing her pajamas, she held out a plate with some toast and butter and a to-go cup of coffee.

He remained still, torn between making that phone call and faking an illness and backing away from the feeling that he *wanted* to have her there every morning.

For a long time.

She rolled her eyes. "Take the damn food, Cathal. It's breakfast, not a proposal of marriage."

He didn't comment on the marriage bit. With Fiona, his hard-fast rule of remaining alone seemed like it belonged to some other man. A man who didn't have a gorgeous woman handing him cold toast and weak coffee.

Without asking or questioning himself, he kissed her. Harder and rougher than a sweet kiss she probably deserved. And she responded, shifting her body until her chest pressed against his.

He dropped his laptop bag to the floor, giving him the freedom to back her up against the refrigerator. She held the coffee and toast out to the side.

Perfect. Nothing between him and her body. His hands molded to her ribcage, wanting to explore but knowing he'd never leave the apartment.

His phone chimed in his pocket.

He broke off the kiss without finesse. "I've got to leave before you tempt me to call in."

"I'm still not ready to sleep with you."

Tracing a finger along the curve of her cheek, he watched the blue in her eyes darken. "Maybe not, but last night proved I'll take whatever you're willing to give me. Even if that's just your warm body pressed against my side for the night."

She pushed the plate and cup into his hand. "Right now, I'm giving you toast and coffee." With a cute little smile, she slapped his butt. "Go to work."

He winked, happy that she smiled back. "I'll catch up with you later." He picked up his messenger bag, took his breakfast, and left. Nice way to start the morning. Better than waking up either hungover or exhausted.

The drive to his office took ten minutes—parking and getting through security another three.

He arrived four minutes late. Mrs. Cabot was crying in the corner. Her soon-to-be-ex sat two chairs away with a nasty edge to his voice, saying something low to her.

She bolted from the chair when she spotted Cathal. "I was afraid you wouldn't come." Her hands were clenched together in front of her.

Cathal sat his hand over hers. Ice cold. He looked over her head at Mr. Cabot. A thin, angry-looking man who Cathal wished he had a chance to deal with in his own way. Fiona's touch, her hand gliding up and down his back the last time he'd gotten angry, flashed through his mind.

He'd control it.

"Is your lawyer here, Mr. Cabot?" he asked.

Mr. Cabot motioned toward the hallway. "He went to the restroom."

"Alright. I'm going to take my client to the conference room. I'll be back out to get you in a few minutes."

"I can't believe you're paying for this shit, Margie. It's not like you're entitled to anything. I earned it all." Mr. Cabot sucked his teeth and sat back, leg crossed over his knee. "Just wait."

Cathal led Mrs. Cabot to the conference room and closed the door. "Why did you just take that from him?"

She turned around, wiping a hand across her eyes. "What do you mean?"

"You're not his wife. Even if the divorce isn't final, you're no longer his wife. Not that he had a right to speak to you before in that manner, but now you can walk away." Or tell him to screw himself, but Mrs. Cabot didn't seem like the type.

"I...I..." She looked around the room like a scared rabbit. He couldn't stand to see someone so beat down. So insecure about themselves. Afraid of their shadow.

He thought of Kami. As much as her constant advances bugged the hell out of him, he was glad to see she wasn't the same woman, like Mrs. Cabot, as she'd been when he represented her. As much as he knew, he helped in these situations, the constant need to restrain himself, swallow down his gut reaction, was beginning to wear him down.

"I have the name of a few therapists that have helped my other clients in the past. I don't get any type of referral fees. They're just specialists that have seen abuse and helped others in your situation. Consider going to see them."

"But that'll cost money." She sat down in a chair, setting

her forehead in her hand. "I don't have any money. I don't even have any skills to get a job."

Cathal patted her on the back before setting his bag in the chair beside her. "Don't worry about the money."

"He won't give me anything."

"We'll see. But, do me a favor, don't downplay the abuse. The other lawyer needs to know the situation. He can't hurt you anymore." He left her with a box of tissues and went to find Mr. Cabot.

He rose with his lawyer when Cathal walked into the room. "Ready?"

Mr. Cabot adjusted his suit jacket. "About damn time. I have a business of my own to run. This is pointless, anyway."

Cathal followed them into the room, taking his seat beside Mrs. Cabot and ignoring the mutterings of the jackass across from him.

"Cathal, let's just make this quick," Samson said. Mr. Cabot's lawyer had represented others against Cathal in the past. They'd never had a contentious mediation, and he hoped Samson would be just as reasonable with this case.

"I'd love to make this quick. She wants the house, eight-thousand a month in support, and another thousand for child support."

Samson sat back. "Mr. Cabot isn't willing to pay more than, um, two thousand."

Cathal raised an eyebrow.

Samson looked away. Yeah, the man knew that was a shit offer.

"She's not worth more than that," Mr. Cabot said, his voice rising higher.

Samson said something low, but that didn't affect the

man. "She's ungrateful. Left me after everything I did for her."

"She was tired of being abused," Cathal replied in a low tone. He set his hands on the desk, trying to appear relaxed. "You know she filed a police report after the last time you visited her. I have the paperwork drawn up for a restraining order against you."

"What proof-"

Cathal cut Samson off. "Was Mrs. Cabot crying when you left them alone a few minutes ago?"

"No."

Cathal looked at Mrs. Cabot. "What did Mr. Cabot do while you were alone?"

Mrs. Cabot shook her head in a small motion.

"This is ludicrous. We're here to settle this shit. I'm not going to sit here and pay my lawyer an hourly wage to watch you disparage my name."

Cathal stared hard at Mrs. Cabot. "I need you to talk about it. What happened?"

"He...he told me that the next time he had...well...Collin that he'd take the belt to him again just to make me cry."

Samson shook his head. "Cathal, seriously, you believe this? Mr. Cabot is president of one of the largest regional banks in the country."

"Which means our demands for spousal and child support aren't beyond reason." Cathal sat back in the chair. "There's a video feed in our waiting area."

"I'm being taped unknowingly!"

"It's a security camera. Almost everywhere you go in Atlanta, you're being taped without your knowledge."

"But you can't confirm what I said."

"It doesn't matter. The fact that you made a point to lean over and say *anything* that made Mrs. Cabot cry and cringe and look like she would shatter if you touched her is enough for me, and it will be enough for the judge. She's supported your ass for the past fifteen years."

Mr. Cabot jerked up, the chair falling backward on the ground. "She hasn't done a damn thing to help me over the years. I worked while she played housewife, raising two kids."

"Exactly." Cathal rose, the edge of his vision blurring. He blinked, clearing the haze. Focus.

Fiona.

Like before, a wave of peacefulness washed over him.

He continued. "She stayed home and supported you. She kept your house. Washed your clothes. Cooked your dinner. Raised your children. She's entitled to half of everything you earned over these years *plus* future support as you left her without the ability to find suitable work for the time being. And support for your two children that you don't even want joint custody of." He raised his eyes to Samson. "I have an abused spouse with two children and no trade or skills, and you have a belligerent husband with a loudmouth." He pulled the sheet of paper he'd set on the table earlier with his conditions back to him. "I can revise this, and we can take the case before a judge. Or, you can talk to your client and get back in touch with us in a week."

Samson sighed and gave Cathal a small, almost imperceptible nod. "We'll be in touch." He rose and motioned Mr. Cabot forward.

Mr. Cabot stopped by Mrs. Cabot.

Cathal stepped in front of him. "Keep moving."

Samson nudged him along, and they left, Mr. Cabot's loud, angry shouts floating in through the open door a second later.

Cathal set a hand on Mrs. Cabot's shoulder. "Are you alright?"

"Do you really think he'll give me eight thousand a month?"

"Yes. Are you sure you don't want to ask for more?"

Mrs. Cabot shook her head. "No. I don't want more. I can have a nice house in the suburbs and live peacefully. That's all I want right now."

He understood. "We won't settle. You'll get everything you need."

Her expression shifted into concern, and she laid a hand on his arm. "Are you alright?"

That was odd. His clients didn't usually worry about him. "Yes. Why do you ask?"

"There was a moment there when it looked like you might lunge across the table at him." Her voice lowered a touch. "I almost wished you had. I know that makes me a terrible person."

Had he? He'd felt in control for the most part. Each time, the brief thought of Fiona had settled him down. He wouldn't dwell on what that meant. Things already felt too heavy and committed between the two of them.

That wasn't the issue. The problem came in the form of the fact it didn't scare him to have her near.

"No. It makes you a normal person that doesn't want to be abused. And thank you for asking, but I'm fine. Once I hear back from them, I'll let you know. Remember, lock your doors and call the police if he comes anywhere close to you in a threatening manner."

She nodded and left the office.

He leaned on the table, letting his head drop forward. This would be the last divorce mediation he took. He didn't know what he'd do, maybe just work at O'Keeley's, but he was done trying to weave around these issues and not have something set him off.

He passed his office without stopping in for messages and left the building. He was no better than part-time anyways. And as much as he wanted to go back to his apartment and see if he could charm Fiona back into bed, he headed toward the restaurant. He had his own lawsuit to deal with.

FIONA VENTURED into O'Keeley's for lunch. Mostly because she hoped to see Cathal and beg him to go to her mom's birthday party with her. She didn't blame him if he refused. Besides, she'd have another huge favor to ask in borrowing a bartender or two to man her bar until she returned.

She spotted Katie at the hostess stand and immediately embraced her when Katie prompted. A friend. God, it was nice to have one again.

"You look ready to make a point." Katie motioned to Fiona's outfit.

Fiona adjusted her top, pulling it up in the front. "I don't need to make *that* much of a point."

Katie shook her head. "If you're here to see Cathal, leave it. I'm sure he'll appreciate the view."

"Is Cathal back yet? I tried his cell phone, but he didn't answer."

"Yes. He got in about an hour ago. In the office."

Fiona smiled again and walked across the restaurant. She paused and knocked on the door.

Kami opened the door, her smile wide as she laughed. She ran Cathal's silk tie, the one he'd worn when he left the apartment that morning, through her hands. "Well, well, look who's here." Kami laid the tie around her neck. "We were just having a laugh about old times."

Cathal stepped behind Kami, his hand propping open the door. The top buttons of his shirt were undone, and he'd rolled up his shirt sleeves. The laugh on his lips died immediately when he saw her.

Fiona's stomach dropped.

"What are you doing here?"

"Making a mistake." She jerked away when he reached around Kami for her.

Turning, she stalked back through the restaurant in a pace just short of being a jog. Why had she thought it'd be different with him?

That he'd be different with her?

She should have known better. Him and Kami looked far too cozy together, alone in his office. And the man had the audacity to ask *her* what she was doing there.

Shit.

She was dumb for thinking—

"Stop." Cathal's hand encircled her upper arm.

Fiona pushed it away. "No." She held her hands up and faced him, walking backward toward the exit. "You don't have anything to explain."

Anger flashed in his eyes.

She'd expected guilt, or even a dumb, flirty wink, but anger? It wasn't the rage she'd seen before, but God, it was close.

"Stop," he said lower, nearly a growl. "If you didn't jump to a damn conclusion, you'd know that nothing is going on."

"With your history, there are a lot of conclusions to jump to." She twisted to keep walking, but he jumped in front of her. "Move."

"No." He stepped closer, his voice still sounding gritty

and deep. "I've done nothing to deserve your mistrust. Come back into the office, please, or I'll have this out with you in front of everyone in the restaurant."

She wiped away a tear, hating it'd even formed.

The fury in his face softened. Slightly. "Come back with me." He kissed her forehead. "If you leave, I'll just run after you."

She huffed, crossed her arms, and followed him back into the office. Right past Kami, who stood behind the bar. Fiona had expected some gloating. She'd managed to score with Cathal after all.

Fiona entered the office, shocked to see Brogan on the sofa with his arm around Selena.

Selena's worried expression said it all.

Fiona had overreacted. She swallowed, her throat dry. Embarrassed didn't begin to describe the emotion churning in her stomach. After their night last night, realizing how much she cared and wanted Cathal, she couldn't get her head on straight.

"First, as you can see, I was not alone with Kami." Cathal's movement was jerky.

Oh, he was seriously pissed off.

She bit her tongue, letting him finish. She'd have to apologize. That made her stomach hurt worse. Pride was all she had left with from her last relationship.

"Second, she came in to tell *all* of us about her ex-husband, the one that I got the divorce settlement from, about his new girlfriend. His new eighty-five-year-old girlfriend. The picture she showed us of them on her yacht was funny since the man who'd abused her wore gold brief swim trunks." Cathal raised an eyebrow.

Her turn. She gripped her hands together, her fingers squeezing tightly. He wouldn't let her off. She knew that.

Brogan and Selena sat quietly on the sofa. Selena grimaced and ducked her chin.

Yeah. She didn't have a choice.

"I'm sorry I jumped to a conclusion about the two of you." She crossed her arms, suddenly feeling cold. Her voice sounded distant. Flat. "But I didn't see Brogan and Selena."

Cathal stepped a little closer, lowering his voice again. "That shouldn't have mattered. I told you that if you were in my apartment, if you were the woman I kissed, held, that I wouldn't be with anyone else. I understand with my history that's a difficult concept, but it's an easy choice for me to make for you, Fiona."

The confidence in his words brought another wave of emotion, and tears stung her eyes. She nodded. "I'm sorry."

He held her chin lightly, tipping up her face to his. His kiss wasn't sweet or tender. It was intense and a little rough. Frustrated with her, no doubt.

Brogan cleared his throat.

Cathal eased back. "Aside from that, I'm glad you stopped by. Did you want lunch?"

The man forgave her so quickly. Her parents, even Hugo, would have held it over her head. Made her feel bad for hours, days, after making such a big mistake.

As it was, she *had* seen Hugo with another woman, and no one gave a shit about her anger.

"I did want lunch. But I had a favor to ask of you as well. Tomorrow night is my mom's birthday party."

"Did you want me to watch the bar while you go?"

She glanced over at Selena and Brogan, who were whispering together, and then focused back on Cathal. "I wanted you to go with me."

His mouth dropped open before shutting again. "Oh. Really."

"Yes."

"What about your bar?"

Fiona shrugged. "That was favor number two. Can I borrow a bartender or two? I'll pay them, of course. And nothing that would leave O'Keeley's in a lurch. But since you've already screened them, and they definitely know how to work a bar—"

Cathal laid a finger over her lips.

She'd been rambling. She hated asking for help.

"I don't have a problem if you ask."

Selena raised her hand. "I can do it."

"No," Brogan and Cathal said at the same time. Brogan patted her knee. "You're a week away. I'll not have you standing on your feet for hours."

She crossed her arms over her large stomach and rolled her eyes. "Fine."

"Katie might do it." Cathal shrugged. "I'll ask her if you'd like."

"I can ask her. I didn't want to take her in case you needed her."

"No." He looked to Brogan. "We don't, do we?"

Brogan shook his head. "Not that I know of."

Cathal slung his arm over Fiona's shoulders. "Now, I'd like the prettiest woman in Atlanta to be my date for lunch."

She held onto his waist. "How did your mediation go this morning?"

His body stiffened, just a little, but she caught it. The muscle in his jaw worked a moment before he smiled. Ah, the cover-up for his emotions. Something had set him off.

She didn't wait for him to answer and gave his waist a squeeze. "Don't worry about it. Let's talk about something else."

He cut his eyes at her. "I'm not sure I like you reading me so well, Fiona."

"Too bad. You're easy to read."

"No one else ever has." He kissed her temple, and then he held out her chair.

Katie walked up, holding out menus. "Welcome to O'Keeley's. Are you on a lunch break from work? We have a few items on the menu that may take a little longer to make."

Fiona sat forward. "Are you busy tomorrow night?"

"Nope. My girlfriend has to work. Why?"

"Can you work at my bar? I'd pay you, obviously."

Katie brightened, running a hand over her white hair with pink tips. "I'd love to. I've always wanted to try and bartend in a real bar."

"Great."

Cathal leaned back, watching her with a curious expression. "Exactly where is your ma's birthday party?"

"Their house."

"Will Hugo be there?"

"Does it matter?"

Cathal picked up her hand, kissing the back of her knuckles. "Not at all."

16

The champagne was Rian's idea. He'd turned into a soft romantic since finding Mara, but Cathal took the advice. He poured two glasses and had them waiting when Fiona stepped out of her room.

Her hair was straight, a style he almost forgot she wore. It was pulled long over one shoulder. Her makeup was subtle with light pink lips. Her dress, also pink, had a tiny black belt at the waist and ended at her knees.

He held out a glass of champagne. "You look beautiful." That was the best he could do. She looked untouchable, like a cookie-cutter housewife in a magazine. That wasn't his Fiona. But she was still gorgeous. He just preferred her wearing an over-sized T-shirt, and her hair tousled from sleep.

Her shoulders slouched, and her head dropped to the side. "That bad, huh?"

Pressing the glass of champagne into her hand, he kept his expression sober. "You're pretty in anything you wear. I'm just partial to you in clothes that I'm not scared to wrinkle."

She took a sip. "Thank you for this. I need some fortification to get through the night."

"It won't be that bad." He wanted to touch her, but he'd been serious. He would mess up all her hard work once he started. "We can finish the bottle of champagne when we get back and celebrate surviving."

"That's a pretty big assumption seeing that we haven't even left the house yet."

"I'm a positive person." He smirked at her bland expression. "Most of the time." He finished his drink and picked up the car keys from the table. He'd endure anything if it meant being there for her. She needed some closure, but he wasn't sure tonight would bring it.

From what he saw of her da, Mr. Grant was determined to fight for his daughter by any means necessary. And Cathal was ready for the attack. He'd make a point to him and the rest of the lot. Fiona was his.

He held the door open for her but stopped her with a hand on her elbow. "I can't stand this. You'll just have to fix your lips again."

Careful not to touch anything else, he brushed his mouth over hers once before sinking into a deep, slow kiss, the taste of champagne heightening every desire for her. It ended quicker than he wanted, but they needed to leave. "There. I might survive."

"That makes one of us." She walked ahead, out of the apartment, and to his car. "Thank you again for coming with me. I might not have gone otherwise. I found out that all my old friends will be there, at Hugo's invitation."

"Your da is dead set on the two of you getting back together, isn't he?"

"Yes." She huffed and crossed her arms.

Cathal thought of her current schedule. Her life. "Fiona, do you have friends?"

She turned her head, staring out the passenger side window. "I used to have a lot of friends. Some I would have considered best friends. But they ran in the same circle as Hugo, and they took his side over mine. I think they all assumed I'd fall in line with my father and him." She turned back. "But I've enjoyed getting to know Mara and Selena. Katie."

Was he her closest friend? The idea pleased him and gave him a jolt of pity. For months he'd wanted Fiona to like him enough to give him the time of day because he liked the chase but knowing that he'd turned into one of her only friends brought him a warmth he'd not expected. Inch by inch, she broke down the wall around his future a little more.

He gripped the steering wheel tight. They should end it before it hurt worse. Something was bound to explode when he screwed it all up. She needed to be far away from him when the fallout happened. She shouldn't start relying on him that way. Anything could happen.

She smiled. He didn't see pain or anger, hurt, nothing but Fiona. "I'm actually happier now than I've been in a long time. Even before the debacle with Hugo and my wedding. And I really enjoyed hanging out with Selena, Mara, and Katie. We talked about going to the movies after Selena had the baby to give her a few hours to herself." She nudged him gently. "Maybe you can babysit."

"I would think the babysitting duties would fall to Brogan."

"I don't think we call a dad watching his child 'babysitting'. It's more like watching your child."

Cathal chuckled. "I suppose you're right. I don't mind babysitting little Rosie; I'd just like her potty trained first."

Fiona's shocked expression looked cute. "That will be years."

"Alright. Then I'll babysit in a few years."

She shook her head. "I bet you won't. I bet you're a softy when it comes to kids."

He didn't respond. Because she was right about him. He loved kids. Always had. But a child was another layer of responsibility that he couldn't risk.

They drove through the Atlanta streets, busy on a Saturday night. Fiona gripped her hands together, bounced her knee, and huffed a few times when she crossed her arms.

He sat his hand on her knee, his thumb stroking her smooth skin. "It'll be alright."

"I know they'll be mean to you. I shouldn't have dragged you into this."

"I'll be happy to endure whatever abuse they can dole out if it makes it easier for you." He tugged her hand free from the death grip she had on the armrest. "Just think about later." He kissed the inside of her wrist, discovering the sweet honeysuckle scent he loved. "We'll go back to the apartment." He kissed her again, enjoying the sound of her breath through her lips when she sighed. "Alone." He stopped at a red light, getting to focus all his attention on her and enjoying the way a flush crawled across her cheeks. "And I'll let you give me another back massage."

She let out a sharp laugh. "I thought you wanted sex."

"I don't want sex until you want sex." The light turned, and he pulled off, interlacing his fingers with hers and setting them on his thigh. He wanted her, right next to him, the entire night.

She settled back in her seat, laying her head back and closing her eyes. "My yoga instructor says we should breathe through the stress. Meditate. Focus on a positive outcome."

"Oh, I completely agree." He brought the inside of her wrist back to his lips. "The positive outcome is that you're coming home with me. No matter what happens."

"My father won't scare you off?"

"Nope." He pulled into a neighborhood with a security gate. In the distance, he could see the first massive house. He wouldn't say a mansion, but it was grander than anything he'd ever been in before. "We're here for the Grant birthday party," he said when the guard approached.

The guard leaned down. "Fiona? Wow. Haven't seen you in a while."

"Hi, Gary." She didn't say his name with much warmth.

Gary shifted, his eyes flicking between the two of them. "What's this? A date? Hugo has already been through here."

"That's nice to know. And yes, this is my date." She sat back and broke eye contact, effectively ending their conversation.

Cathal smiled politely and waited for Gary to open the iron gate for him to enter the neighborhood. Fiona was born into this lifestyle. The pretty dresses, fancy shoes, sleek hair. Expectations and guilt. But anyone that knew her saw she was miserable.

He'd do his best to make sure that she survived, if not enjoyed herself. She'd brought him a modicum of peace he'd never experienced with any other woman.

Cathal stopped the car at the end of a long driveway. "Do you want me to drive up and drop you off, so you don't have to walk in those shoes?"

Fiona reached in the backseat and pulled out a small, robin's egg blue bag. "No. I'm fine. Just park down there."

He did as she asked, and within a few steps out of the car, he reached for her hand. A few men stood on the front porch of the house, watching them approach. Fiona kept her head down, staring at the ground. She'd shown up to support her ma.

He'd come along to make sure she had the support she needed.

It was a perk that he could show everyone in her family's inner circle that she was with him. For the night, for the month, however long it lasted, she was his.

When they reached the bottom of the driveway, *exactly* where their audience had a perfect view, he tugged her close.

"Let me have one more kiss before this night starts." He kissed her without waiting for an answer. She didn't shy away, which encouraged him. Her arms wrapped around his neck as her body molded against his. He had a hell of a lot to figure out, but for the night, everyone would damn well know which man she'd go home with.

"Hold on to me, I'll help you up the driveway," he said, giving his mind something else to think of besides wanting to throw her over his shoulder and cart her back to his apartment.

"Thank you." She linked her arm through his elbow and started up the steep driveway.

As expected, the seven men standing on the porch watched them approach.

"Great. Hugo is out as a part of the welcoming committee," she mumbled under her breath. "Why can't my parents just be normal?"

"If your parents were normal, you wouldn't have ended up in my apartment, so I'm thankful. This where you grew up?"

"Yes." She pointed at a window on the left, second story. "That's my room." She pulled him a little closer, her breast brushing against his arm, her voice taking on a teasing, suggestive tone. "We can go look at it later if you want."

"Absolutely," he snapped out quick enough that it made her laugh. He'd try to keep her happy all night, even dealing with her family shit.

"Dad," Fiona said as she stepped away from Cathal to hug her da. "Hi."

"I see you remember where we live." Mr. Grant put his hands in his pockets, purposefully avoiding shaking Cathal's hand. That didn't bother him. He wasn't too keen to shake the man's hand anyway.

Another older gentleman stepped forward and held out his hand. "I'm Ned, Fiona's uncle."

Cathal shook his hand, liking the man's demeanor immediately. "Cathal O'Keeley. Nice to meet you."

"Are you Irish?"

"Yes. Grew up in Roscommon."

Ned nodded his head, looking genuinely interested. Nice to have a friendly face. "I always enjoy traveling there. Have you ventured anywhere else in Europe?"

"Me? No." He shook his head, keeping a hand firmly around Fiona's waist as she spoke in low, clipped words with her da. "My brother is the traveler in our family. He's a chef."

Fiona stepped back close to his side. "He just cooked lunch for Mom and Dad the other day. It was delicious."

"What's his name?" Ned asked.

"Rian O'Keeley."

Ned's eyes widened a touch. It was the only outward sign that he'd been impressed with the name. "Oh. Yes. I've heard of him."

Hugo spoke from his spot against the railing of the front porch. "Is he prone to violence as well?"

Fiona's breath sucked in through her teeth.

Cathal didn't let it get to him. He'd assumed that someone would find out about his past. He readjusted his hand on Fiona's waist.

"No. Rian's more level-headed than either my older brother or myself."

"I wonder if you've informed Fiona of your past transgression? It might change how she sees you. It worries *me* a little with her living so close to you."

Cathal debated how to handle the question. He wanted to threaten Hugo, get in his face, show him exactly how violent he could be, but that wouldn't help Fiona. Plus, with her hand absently stroking his lower back, he could take a deep breath and let the sharp stab of rage ease away.

"Yes. She does know about my past." Cathal leaned closer, dropping his voice, so her da and uncle were left out. "But she's not scared of me. I think *my* Fiona enjoys knowing what I'd gladly do to any man who ever hurt her."

Hugo's pupils dilated in his pale blue eyes, but other than that, he held perfectly still.

Fiona tugged on Cathal's arm. "I can't wait to see Mom. Let's *go.*"

He let her lead him away, his eyes still locked with Hugo's. That was the side of him he didn't trust. That side would get him in trouble and bring Fiona down with him. He cared too much for the woman to do that to her.

"Wow," she murmured.

Cathal glanced down at her, curious. "What?"

She bit down on her lower lip. "That was stupidly sexy what you just said to him." She cut her eyes, punctuating her words. "I don't want you to fight but being on the receiving end of your protective streak is a new feeling for me."

"I meant it."

Fiona gazed up at him. "I did, too." With that, she walked through the doorway to the living room. A massive space that would have encompassed his entire cottage growing up.

The gold and crystal chandelier caught the light from the twenty or so candles lit around the room. All the French doors along the far side of the room were open, letting the guests flow smoothly to the bar set up along the terrace. The entire area seemed to be various shades of beige and gold. Bland but opulent.

Somehow, the vibrant woman who squeezed his hand came from this museum.

"Mom," Fiona said, giving her ma a warm hug. "The house looks great!"

Mrs. Grant scanned the room. "I had no idea your father invited so many people. It makes me feel truly blessed to have everyone with me to celebrate my birthday." She held her arms wide. "Along with you, Cathal." She hugged him. "I'm glad you could come."

"I'm happy to be invited."

A string quartet began warming up, the music floating in through the open doors.

Mrs. Grant waved her hand toward the terrace. "That was also your father's idea. He's gone all out for this party." She patted Fiona's shoulder. "I think it's for you as much as for me."

"Why?" Fiona shifted toward Cathal.

He set a hand on her waist.

"He's hoping you'll reconnect with your friends, this life, and want to come back. I know he and Hugo both need you at the company." Her mom appeared oblivious to Fiona's reaction. The way she withdrew, her smile turning wooden, her body stiff and warmer than usual.

She tilted her chin up and took in a large breath of air. "I'm sorry he made the effort."

Her mom's happy expression dropped immediately. "Oh, dear, I've upset you."

Fiona shook her head. "No. You haven't. Let's just celebrate you today. Is that alright?" She held out the little blue bag. "I brought you a present."

"Oh!" She took the bag. "You really shouldn't have. And from Tiffany's!" She dug into the gift, pulling out a long box. Mrs. Grant held up a silver bracelet with small stones in a variety of colors. "It's so pretty. And will be perfect with summer right around the corner." She kissed Fiona's cheek. "Thank you."

"You're welcome." She remained rigid until her mom moved away. Finally, her body relaxed back against Cathal's chest. "Think I can leave yet?"

Cathal chuckled low, leaned down, and kissed her cheek. "We'll make it. Then you can walk away from all this grandeur a second time."

She scanned the room, her soft hair brushing against his jaw. "I've never stood in this room and felt so uncomfortable before. Empty."

He set his hand on the back of her neck, squeezing her tense muscles gently. "Your life has changed. Nothing's wrong with that."

"The gift to my mom costs twenty thousand dollars."

"You just spent-"

"Their own money. They set up an account for me when I left. In case I needed it. They officially have nothing to hold over me." She faced him, shrugging as she held out her arms. "I'm on my own now."

No. She wasn't. She had him, but he smiled and covered up the rush of emotions. "Let's get a drink and check out the band."

"Band? It's a string quartet."

"And right now, that seems more exciting than your parents' friends." He set his arm around her shoulder, and they walked out onto the terrace. "I would have brought my fiddle had I known. Could have livened things up a bit."

"I forgot you play the fiddle. Maybe you'll play for me sometime."

Two women, Fiona's age, stood at the bar, accepting a glass of champagne.

The tall one, over six feet, stopped mid-sentence. "Oh, my God! Fiona!" She opened her arms and rushed forward with a squeal. "I cannot believe that you came!"

Fiona hugged her. "Kerri. Hi. It is my mom's birthday party. Why wouldn't I?"

The other one, a woman with brown hair pulled back into a ponytail, stayed back at the bar.

"Wren?" Fiona stepped around Kerri. "I'd think it would be more of a shock that you came."

This was the woman who'd slept with Hugo. She was pretty, to be sure, but plain compared to Fiona.

"Now, Fiona, let's not start anything." Kerri edged herself between Wren and Fiona. "She was invited, just like the rest of us. We're all hoping that you'll move on. We miss seeing you."

"I'm thirty minutes away." Fiona crossed her arms. "And since no one even bothered to call me in the past year, I can't imagine you miss me all that much."

"Hugo didn't want us to."

Kerri's admission brought Fiona's shoulders back, her

blue, fairy eyes narrowing into slits. Cathal stepped forward, trying to diffuse the bomb he saw brewing.

"Hi, I'm Cathal O'Keeley." He shook Kerri's hand and then Wren's. He pointed at their glasses of champagne. "Do you know if they have anything else to drink?"

"You're Irish," Kerri said. People always sounded so shocked when he spoke. It usually amused him. Right then, his concern was for Fiona.

He didn't respond to the question. "Fiona, darling, what do you want to drink? Champagne?"

Fiona's eyes snapped away from Wren's. "No. I suddenly can't stand the stuff."

He grinned and rubbed his hands together. "Alright. Let's see what they have."

"Fiona, we have to talk about this at some point." Wren gave her a sympathetic look that probably wouldn't go over very well. "We have the same friends-"

"Friends? We've managed to avoid each other for the past year easily. I don't see why that needs to change." Fiona's gaze swept around the terrace. "If this is what you wanted when you slept with Hugo, this life, these *friends,* then you are more than welcome to them. In fact, I should thank you for bringing me to my senses. I wasn't in love with Hugo."

"Excuse me, do you have any beer?" Cathal asked the bartender, keeping an eye on Fiona's heated cheeks.

Wren's shoulders straightened. "Then it makes it easier to tell you that Hugo and I have been seeing each other for the past year while you've been gone."

Fiona's fairy eyes narrowed into slits.

"Whiskey?" Cathal changed his order. "Please tell me you have some whiskey behind that bar."

Fiona expression shifted into something Cathal didn't

expect. Sympathy. "Wren, you need to leave Hugo. He and my father are determined for me to go through with marrying him. He wouldn't do that if he loved you."

"I don't believe you." Wren shook her head and drank the champagne in one large gulp. "Hugo loves me. Not you."

The bartender set two glasses of whiskey on the countertop. Cathal didn't even care what brand at that point. He pushed a glass into Fiona's hand.

Kerri giggled in a fake, high-pitched tone. "I think we need to plan to do lunch. Clear the air. We've all been friends for so long, this shouldn't come between us. What about lunch next Wednesday?"

"No," Fiona said before tossing back the whiskey. It'd been a double pour, not meant to be a shot. She thrust her hand out to Cathal.

He took the glass and set it on the counter, waiting to see what her next move would be.

Nothing.

She turned and walked away.

Cathal followed her into the house and past her mother, who waved and smiled at him. "Where are we headed, darling?" He heard pans clanging and a rise of voices as he spotted the kitchen, but Fiona turned right and headed up a set of stairs in the back of the house.

Three doors down the hallway, she opened one.

A bedroom. The pale-yellow curtain over the large window cast a soft glow into the room with the setting sun. A white bedspread covered a large, king-sized bed with four tall posters in the same cherry wood as the dresser.

"This was my room."

Cathal leaned against the doorway, watching her walk into the vast space. "I have to say; your room was a little nicer than mine growing up."

"And yet, you probably had more love than I've ever known."

Her whispered words sent a shiver over his skin.

"I wanted to see it one last time."

"What do you mean?" He moved into the room, set his whiskey glass on the dresser, and turned her to face him. "You can still reconcile with your parents."

"There's not one person in this house that's tried to see me. Call me. Find out if I'm even alright. Everyone sided with Hugo, and they can have him." She wrapped her arms around her stomach.

His heart broke.

"I shouldn't have come here. To see it, realize that no one that I grew up with, my family, no one in this house, gives a shit hurts worse than ignoring it. I thought I was the one who'd left. I was the one in charge. All along, it'd been a one-sided fight."

Cathal reached out, gripping her hip with one hand, the back of her neck with the other, pulling her against him. "I care." He kissed her. "More than I should let myself." Because for him, it led to a dead end.

She held onto his shoulders. "Just shut up."

17

When had she fallen in love with Cathal?

It didn't matter. Right then, she needed him, and she'd take as much as he'd give her. She pulled him into a deep kiss. It broke through the pain. The self-doubt. Most of all, it shattered the heartache caused by her family.

She couldn't focus on anything or anyone else. Not with the feel of his body or the taste of the whiskey.

He backed her up until the poster of the bed stopped her.

It gave him leverage, leaving his hands free to roam along the curves of her body before tracing down her hips. He bunched her skirt in his fists and mumbled her name. Her stomach tightened at the passion in his voice.

She had Cathal. He was a better man than any other man in her life, even with his past.

And his family, his friends, had accepted her. She wasn't alone. It might not last, but for the moment, she had people in her life who cared. She'd hold onto that and let the rest go.

"I want you," he said, pausing in his kiss. His breath

fanned across her cheek. "And I wish it could be right now." His hands tightened again. "You're killing me."

She didn't want her first time with him in her childhood bedroom. Rushed. She nipped at his lower lip. "We should probably get back."

He nodded and stepped away. The dark look in his eyes, the intensity that he only revealed to her, confirmed his desire. Most of the time, she saw Cathal, every facet, the dark, and the light. But right then, she saw him as others would. His dark hair, blue eyes. Insanely attractive, especially all buttoned up in his suit.

"Yeah, let's get back or stop looking at me that way."

"You're hot. It's hard not to look sometimes."

He ran a hand over his hair. Everything about him shifted. Back to the Cathal he presented to the world. A flirty, happy playboy. He grinned and pointed to her dress. "I ended up wrinkling you, after all."

Sighing, she adjusted her dress and checked her makeup in the mirror over the dresser. She hated that change in him, but she understood it.

"I'm going to do one more lap around the party, and then we leave."

He set his hands on either side of her, watching her in the mirror. "I hope you'll do me the honors of helping you out of this dress later." He kissed a sensitive spot where her neck met her shoulder, keeping his eyes on hers.

It was amazing that the dress didn't unzip itself.

She turned within his arms and patted his chest, giving him a slight shove backward. "We need to get back to the party."

"So, you've said that." He rubbed a hand over his chin, watching her with a cute smirk. "Fiona, darling, you're going to be the death of me."

She patted him on the chest again as she passed by, glad for the distraction. "I think you'll survive."

"Possibly, but it will be a painful existence."

He followed her back to the party, staying close by her side. A few curious glances were shot toward him, which didn't surprise her. He was by far the best-looking man in the house. She managed a glimpse of the bemused expression on his face.

Nothing fazed him.

"One lap."

He tilted his head toward her, his blue eyes narrowing. "Let's go so we can help each other get out of these restrictive clothes."

She laughed. "I'm not sure that will happen tonight. I need to go close down the bar, so that may have to wait."

Cathal kissed her temple. "I'm going to go get something to drink for us. Again."

"Thanks." She let him leave. He'd turned into a security blanket. She could do this. She could stand in the living room she grew up in and wait for him to return.

Except now, Wren *with* Hugo, were both headed her way. Wren linked her arm through Hugo's elbow.

He moved to the side, causing her to drop her hand or be pulled off balance.

Why didn't she see that he was just using her? Fiona crossed her arms, forcing herself to keep watching them and not look for Cathal. He'd return soon.

"You two really do look good together." Fiona enjoyed the surprise flutter across Hugo's face. Such a fake asshole. "Wren already told me you're still sleeping with her."

Hugo glanced at Wren with a sharp look. "She lied. I've never once considered myself not engaged with you. That's more than you can say, moving in with another man as you've done."

The pain in Wren's face hurt Fiona. They had been friends once. "Please, Hugo. Just knock it off. I may not like Wren, but I sure as hell believe her over you on this."

"It doesn't matter." He waved his hand like he shooed a fly away. "We're a good fit, Fiona. You and me. That's why I think you deserve an apology."

Her mouth dropped open, and she stared at him, not blinking. Not thinking. Just...Hugo...apologizing?

"It seems as though you've shocked my girlfriend, Hugo. What exactly are you apologizing for? Trying to convince her she's crazy or sleeping with Wren?" Cathal pressed a second glass of whiskey into her hand. "You might need to sip this one."

She did, taking a tiny drink and not taking her gaze from Hugo.

Hugo stepped close to Cathal, pointing his finger in his face.

Cathal didn't budge. Didn't react. Stood there, looking like some *GQ* magazine cover in his suit, one hand in his pocket, the other wrapped around his high-ball glass.

"I would have Fiona back in my life if it weren't for you." He poked Cathal in the chest. "You aren't good enough for her. You never will be." He lowered his voice. "You're still just a murderer."

Wren gasped.

Fiona stepped to get between him and Cathal, but Cathal's arm shot out, blocking her even though he never stopped watching Hugo.

"You're right. I'm not good enough for Fiona. But neither are you. I don't know one man that I think worthy of that woman. He may not exist because we're all shit when we get down to it." Cathal glanced around at the crowd forming, watching the two men. He settled those dark blue, intense eyes back on Hugo. "We're here to celebrate her ma's birthday. But if you speak to her again, if you make her uncomfortable or upset one more time, we're leaving. She doesn't deserve this treatment. Not from someone who once claimed to have loved her."

Fiona locked eyes with her dad, standing to the side of the drama unfolding in their living room. He was to blame for this entire situation. But her life, the way it'd turned out, finding Cathal helping him. She wouldn't change anything.

"Cathal," she said, her voice even and low.

He held Hugo's furious stare for another moment before facing her. "Yes?"

"Take me home."

Cathal's messy apartment was more a home than the cold palace she'd grown up in. She didn't wait for a response. He'd follow her out the door if she left. Spotting her mother in the corner with a girlfriend, oblivious to what'd happened, she walked out, past her father, past the twenty of her not-so-close friends.

She felt Cathal's presence behind her before his hand slipped around her elbow to help her down the steep driveway.

"Are you alright?" How had Hugo's comment affected him?

"Me? You're the one that had to walk out of your ma's party." After leading her to his car, he paused before opening her door. "I meant what I said. There's not a man I know that's worthy of being with you."

She cupped his cheek, knowing what he'd say.

"Especially me."

Silly man. He had no idea of his worth. To her. To his family. But he wouldn't listen to her. "I'm happier than I've been in a long time, so that does have worth. Let's grab some fast food and go back to the apartment and change. I need to see if Katie wants me to come in and close down the bar for her." And she needed to figure out precisely what it'd take for Cathal to understand how much she needed him in her life.

Fiona had gone to bed after taking a shower. Both of which he'd silently wished to be invited to, but that never happened. His mind raced, and sleep would be a while yet. Hugo's comment about his past bothered him more than he'd admit.

Because what he'd said was true. He'd kill another man without a second thought if they hurt Fiona.

And he'd have no remorse.

He closed his eyes. He could always start researching for a way out of the lawsuit again. He'd asked for consultations from a variety of lawyers he knew from Georgetown spread out across the country. They gave him a few ideas, but nothing definitive. It was such a new area that there weren't many cases to review as precedent. That meant he was going to either take the fall or get creative. Inspiration had yet to strike.

Fiona's door opened. Her eyes squinted in the light.

"Are you alright?" he asked, glad to see her hair back to its natural state.

"No. I can't sleep."

"Seems to be a common thing in this apartment. Would you like a drink?"

She shook her head. "Do you mind if we do something to get my mind off of tonight?"

"We can revisit the idea of sharing a shower if you'd like."

She smiled softly and pointed at the TV. "I meant to watch something. It's only eleven. I'm not used to going to bed this early."

"Katie said she could close down the bar." And Cathal had agreed. Katie was more than competent to handle Fiona's bar. "TV it is." He patted the sofa. "What types of shows do you watch?"

"I'm never home Saturday night, so I have no idea."

When she sat on the other end, he moved closer until their legs touched. "Much better."

"Yes." She laid her head on his shoulder. "It is. By the way, Wren called me a few minutes ago."

He slowly scanned the channels on the TV, keeping the volume low. "I thought I heard your phone ring. I figured it was old Hugo trying his luck again. Did she have anything interesting to say?"

"Yes. And I believe her, before you ask. Turns out, Hugo and my dad are the ones who've tried to get me shut down."

Cathal set the remote down. It didn't surprise him. Nor did it surprise her based on her calm tone. "Is that why you can't sleep?"

"Yes. Partly. I knew they didn't like my choice, they wanted me back, but that seems so shady and underhanded. Wren apologized." She half-laughed. "And not in the shitty way Hugo did."

He set his hand on her knee. "I'm sorry, Fiona. I wish I could make it disappear for you."

"I'm more worried my bar will disappear. I hope, after tonight, they will give up. But what if they don't?" She picked her head up and looked at him. "What if they keep trying to shut it down, and eventually they do? I can't fight them both."

"Then you'll open another bar."

"That simple, huh?" She twisted her lips to the side like she didn't believe him. "Just open a new bar."

"Yup." He patted her leg and placed a kiss on her cheek. "It is that easy. Because you want it."

She sighed and laid her head back on his shoulder. "I learned at a young age you don't get what you want."

"That's when other people are in charge of giving things to you. Fiona, you already started a successful bar once. If it gets shut down, you can do it again. And again. You're in charge of your future. Damn, but I sound like one of those ads for the misguided youth on television, don't I?"

She patted his leg. "Yes, but you're much cuter."

He tilted her head back and sank into a long kiss before quickly pulling back. Tonight wasn't for that. She needed the company, not him pushing himself into her bed. But he didn't want to be alone.

No other woman would hear that admission. "Can I stay with you tonight? Not how you think, just sleep-"

"Of course." She didn't watch him with pity. He would have hated that. But the understanding, acceptance in her expression relaxed him. "You can sleep with me every night if you'd like."

Every night. That sounded like a permanent arrangement that he wished he had the chance to accept. But, for now, he'd take what she offered: company in the darkness.

F iona took advantage of the gym in Cathal's apartment building. It cleared her head and gave her a chance to calm down about their relationship. Five days since her mom's party. Five nights that Cathal had held her tight and slept in her bed.

Slept.

He'd rested all night and been wide awake during the day and happy. Mostly. Now and then, something would put the dark, haunted look in his eyes, but not nearly as often as before.

Grabbing a glass of water, she started opening cabinets in Cathal's apartment, looking for cleaning supplies. She found a bottle of glass cleaner that looked like he'd purchased it nearly two decades ago. The cleaning wipes under the kitchen counter were dry. She opened a box from her apartment, one that had sat to the side alongside Cathal's boxes from college and found a half-full bottle of cleaning spray.

She'd make do.

But first, she stripped her bed and threw the sheets into

the wash. She had no intention of being Cathal's maid, but seeing as she was staying rent-free, she needed to feel useful.

After cleaning the kitchen, the living room, and guest bathroom, she stared at the closed door to his room. The last room for her to touch. Would he hate her for venturing in there?

What could the man possibly have in there?

She turned the knob and pushed open the door.

Shit.

Did he have a rug down on the floor, or did he have to use his clothes? How did he own anything clean to wear? The floor of his bedroom looked like a preteen girl's room. T-shirts. Jeans. Sweatpants. Undershirts. Towels. His dang suit!

It was a little ridiculous. His bed was unmade. Well, maybe she could call it made since the only thing on there was a fitted sheet. The flat sheet and comforter were on the other side of the bed, filling up the floor space between the king-sized bed and the wall.

She took a step and then stopped. Was he going to kill her for doing this? No. He might yell, but he'd get over it, and he'd have a clean room in the process. He'd taken her in without hesitation; she could at least try to help.

Starting with the sheets, she made piles, little mounds, that led from the laundry closet through the living room and to his door. Piles of clothes sorted and waiting their turn in the washer. She also found a hamper that had a few of his other suits piled in. She'd take that to the dry cleaners on her way out.

At least it wasn't dirty. She didn't find any food or trash in his room. No women that he'd brought back to his place and then got lost under two months' worth of dirty clothes.

And thank God she hadn't found any women's clothing. She knew he'd had a *very* active life before their relationship began, but that might have set her off.

Three hours later, Fiona sat down on the sofa with a plate of food she'd scavenged from his kitchen and the remote in her hand. She had a couple hours before she had to open the bar.

Was Cathal still at the law firm, or had he gone to O'Keeley's? He didn't have to check in with her, but she was curious. He had a strong work ethic, an intense love for his family, and a selflessness that she'd never seen before. When laid out before her, she didn't have a choice *but* to fall in love with him.

She just had to make sure he didn't run away when she told him.

~

BROGAN SAT on the edge of the sofa. "Did you find out anything about our situation?"

Before Cathal could answer, the door to the office opened, and Rian walked in with Mara.

Brogan straightened and shoved his hands into his suit pockets. "Never mind. We can talk later."

Rian hesitated, but it was Mara who must have caught the drift of the private conversation. "Let me go check on Selena. I saw her sitting at a table, rolling silverware." She kissed Rian on the cheek and left.

The door closed behind her, and Rian snapped his head around. "What's going on?"

"The lawsuit," Cathal said, shifting in the leather chair and feeling uncomfortable anyway. He'd tried not to start drinking so early in the day. Sleeping so well, tightly tucked in beside Fiona, left him less antsy for a drink. Now, he didn't know what to do with his hands. Odd feeling.

"I thought you weren't worried about that." Rian sat down in the second leather chair, shifting his gaze between the two brothers. "What's changed?"

"Nothing." Brogan narrowed his eyes at Cathal.

No. Cathal wouldn't leave Rian in the dark. Brogan would have to chew his ass for it later.

"We saw the tapes from the bar the night the man was served."

Rian's eyes widened. "The tape that you told the judge you didn't have?"

"Yes."

Rian looked to Brogan. "You let him lie? He can lose his license."

"I don't want my license anyway. I'm trying to figure out that part of my life on top of every other crazy thing going on. But I told Brogan, and you, that I'd handle this."

"Yes. File some paperwork, don't go to prison by lying." As the words left his mouth, Rian sat back. "What else have you kept from me?"

He knew. Maybe Cathal's expression gave him away. Or maybe Rian just knew his brothers to know they'd never do anything illegal without good reason.

"The tape showed Selena serving the man."

Rian stood up and started pacing. "Shit. That's not good, is it?"

Cathal held his hands out. "I don't know. There's been so little precedent; it will be up to the judge to decide what to do."

"But she's pregnant. Surely they wouldn't send her to jail."

"No." Cathal shook his head, knowing she wouldn't go. "They wouldn't, but, possibly, she'd have to stand trial."

Rian stopped. "In her condition?"

Cathal shrugged. He didn't know. "But the judge will never find it out."

"Oh." Rian leaned against the wall, watching Brogan. "What are you going to do?"

"He's not doing a damn thing," Cathal said. "Selena needs him. This business needs him. He's going to stay, run the business, and raise our Rosie."

Rian stared at Cathal, slowly shaking his head. "There has to be another way than for you to try and take the fall for this."

"I've looked-"

Brogan leaned on the back of the sofa again, his eyes dark and intense. "Then keep looking. Ask more lawyers. I understand you're willing to take the fall for my wife. I appreciate it more than I could ever tell you. But like I said before, don't do it unless there is absolutely no other way out."

"What about Fiona?" Rian asked. "Have you told her what you're planning on doing?"

Cathal barked out a sarcastic laugh. "Have I told Fiona that I plan to go back to jail if necessary? At least ruin my name? No. I've decided to keep that out of my relationship. It won't last much longer anyway."

"Why?" Rian looked to Brogan and back to Cathal. "What the hell else have I missed?"

"How can you, of all people, even ask me that? I'm glad you found someone to move on with, but you know that won't happen for me. I've accepted it, even though now, after finding Fiona, it will hurt like shit to walk away. But it doesn't matter. I will walk away. Or shove her away.

Whichever one I have to do to put her at a distance." He wanted to knock the smirk off Rian's face. "Now, what's your problem?"

"I'm not the one with a problem. Loving a woman and not knowing what to do with the feelings, that's your problem, brother. I know how to love Mara."

"And you suddenly think I'm in love with Fiona?" Because he was. Damn it, he should never have let her get this far.

"I know you're in love with her." Rian took long, slow steps across the floor. He set a hand on Cathal's shoulder, giving him a light squeeze. "Try. Try to find a different way. Not just for Fiona, but for us all." He gave Cathal a rare hug, pounding on his back. "Go home. Get some sleep."

Cathal grinned, even though the uncertainty of the trial and his future were like ghosts, trailing along behind his thoughts. "I've actually slept better in the past five nights than I have since I was eighteen."

Rian and Brogan shared another look.

"As much as I don't want either of you in my sex life, that's not even happening between Fiona and me."

Again, Rian and Brogan shared a different kind of look.

Brogan looked pensive. "Do you want to talk about it?"

"No. I'm fine. It's just that I've been sleeping in the bed with Fiona, nothing else, and I *can* sleep. With her beside me, I sleep. It's easier. Effortless. Peaceful for the first time in years."

"Me, too," Rian admitted, glancing between the two of them. "Having Mara there, when the memories wake me up, makes them go away quicker."

Brogan's shoulders sagged. "I'm happy for the both of you. Really. I know how hard life has been. But I have to say, I'm a touch jealous."

"Why? You've had Selena in your apartment for months. Almost a year, isn't it? Surely, having her beside you is nicer than sleeping alone," Cathal said.

"Just wait. If either one of you ends up with a pregnant wife who has three days until her due date, you won't sleep worth a shit either. The woman can't get comfortable and feels the need to wake me up to inform me of *her* lack of sleep. She eats, in the bed, in the middle of the night, not caring how loud she crunches on her crackers. And, the one time I kindly suggested she eat in the kitchen, I got my ass chewed out for an hour for not being supportive. I have to imagine that dealing with a screaming infant all night long will be a little easier than Selena and her moody... Hey!"

The door to the office opened, Selena waddling in with Mara beside her.

Cathal chuckled. "Just think of Rosie." But the love he saw on Brogan's face for Selena had wiped away his earlier complaints. "I'm going to head out and work on the lawsuit."

Cathal gave Selena a kiss on the top of her head, hugged Mara, and left. He might never experience what Brogan had described, a wife, a pregnant wife by his side, but at least for the night, he'd sleep soundly beside Fiona.

But before he met her at her bar to help her finish up, he'd spend a few hours working on a way out of the lawsuit.

19

F iona unlocked the apartment door. Cathal hadn't come to the bar. Hadn't called or texted. In fact, she'd not heard from him at all since he left to go to work. She supposed that was how most committed relationships worked. They'd leave for work and meet back at home together. It was new territory since she'd only seriously dated Hugo, and they'd worked in the same company together.

Would he still be awake at almost three in the morning? Part of her hoped not. He'd slept so well the past few days.

Cathal sat in the living room, like before, papers spread across the coffee table. He looked up when she walked in and then looked at his watch. He stood suddenly, the paper in his lap falling to the floor.

"Damn it! I lost track of time." He crossed to her. "You should have called me. I would have-"

She kissed him, mostly to shut him up. "I'm fine. Are you working on the lawsuit again?" The pile of papers had grown over the past few days. "Or divorce?"

He ran a hand over his hair, the muscles in his bicep

jumping with the action. "Lawsuit. I made a promise to Brogan, and I'm trying to iron out the details. If it's even possible. How was your day? Thank you for cleaning my room, by the way. You didn't have to do that." His smile looked a little sheepish. "I know that wasn't an easy task."

What promise had he made to Brogan? The secret between them bothered her. "My day was fine, and I didn't mind. I wasn't sure what I would find."

"Dirty clothes?"

"Thankfully, only your dirty clothes."

He ran a hand over her head and rested it on her shoulder. "I've never invited a girl back to my place, so if you found any female clothing, I'd be just as surprised as you are."

"I don't know how you had anything clean to wear."

He chuckled. "Maybe that was my strategy. End up with the excuse to walk around naked and hope you take advantage of me."

Oddly, she probably would have. Spending the night each night, curled up against him in his arms, had become a test of her perseverance. She wanted him. As her boyfriend. As her lover. But stepping across that line and trusting him scared the hell out of her.

"How did the mediation go on the divorce case? You had that today, too, right?"

He propped his hands on his hips. "I have some news about that. I've decided this will be my last divorce case."

She held onto his waist, his skin warm and muscles tight. The corners of his eyes looked pinched from either exhaustion or pain. "Why?"

"I—I can't handle it." His chest rose with a deep breath. "I don't know what I'll do, but I'm tired of fighting against myself every step. There might not be anything I can do other than avoid the circumstances. And this one has been a sheer strength of mental control over my anger at the son of a bitch involved."

She flattened her hands along the side of his waist and gave him a gentle shake. "I think you're stronger than you give yourself credit for. Don't throw away your career-"

"Stop it," he snapped out, blue eyes sharp. "Don't try to tell me it will get better. It hasn't." He stared at a spot over her shoulder. "It won't. And I'll just drag you down eventually. The sooner you leave, the easier it'll be for both of us, Fiona."

The quick trip of her heart recovered just as fast. His hands fisted by his sides. The muscle in his cheek jumped, and she swore she heard his teeth grind together.

Everything inside of her broke for him.

She reached down and held onto his fist. She pried it open and brought his palm to her lips. His eyes flashed to hers.

"You're more than this, Cathal."

"This needs to end. I told you that at the beginning. I'm not a good bet. I *will* screw up again. You can't fix me."

She placed his open palm over her heart. She wouldn't leave. Couldn't. Not if that was his only reason for pushing her away. It didn't scare her.

"I'm not fixing you. This is me loving you."

His jaw squeezed tighter. His eyes, incredibly blue, filled with emotion and shock.

Fiona tugged his head down to hers, kissing him with everything inside. She loved him. She'd just told him that. He didn't reject her outright. The kiss intensified until her head spun, and her legs grew weak. She clung to him for support, and he held her flush against his taut muscles. Her curves against his edges.

The same as their personality.

He pulled her as he stepped backward and toward his bedroom, his lips never letting up in their assault. She tasted the raw edge of his pain.

Reluctance.

Need.

She needed him just as much. He was made up of so much more than his past. She'd stay with him until he believed it. And she had no doubt she was up against a fight with the stubborn Irishman.

Cathal led her to his bed, sitting down and pulling her into his lap to straddle him. This was happening. She had no desire to leave his bedroom tonight.

"I want you, Fiona," he whispered against her neck a moment before his teeth grazed over a sensitive spot. "Stay."

She nodded and launched back into a kiss that rocked them both and left them breathless. His hands had her shirt off and bra unsnapped in the next second. He had a hell of a lot more experience at this than she did. What if she didn't live up to his expectations?

He leaned back, watching her with the intensity she'd felt in his kiss. "What?"

"Nothing." She tried to bring his mouth back to hers and ignore the insecurity creeping into her brain, but he held her at a distance.

"No. What is it? You stiffened. Something changed."

She didn't want to talk about it. "Are you always so concerned about your partner?"

He stood, her legs wrapping around him instantly. He held her up, turned, and fell onto the bed with her. "No. Just you. If you aren't going to tell me, then I'm going to try my hardest to make you forget."

"Forget about what?"

"Everything." A wicked grin replaced his serious expression. "This is about to be fun."

"Cathal—" Her words cut off when his mouth trailed down over her breast.

Fun. Right.

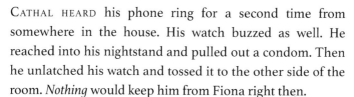

CATHAL HEARD his phone ring for a second time from somewhere in the house. His watch buzzed as well. He reached into his nightstand and pulled out a condom. Then he unlatched his watch and tossed it to the other side of the room. *Nothing* would keep him from Fiona right then.

The woman was full of soft curves that molded under his hands. Part of his mind tried to compare her to the rest of the women he'd been with. But it couldn't. No other woman had ever released fire in his blood before the way she had. The want. The need. Every inch of him had to have Fiona.

And he took her.

Finally, he pushed into her. Colors and lights flickered behind his eyes as he squeezed them tight.

Then he was lost. In her body. The feel of her breath across his neck. The sound of his name.

It wrecked him.

He loved it. He loved her. The one pure, simple thought rammed into his heart as he collapsed on top of her.

Their bodies were damp with sweat. Their hearts pounded against each other.

Fiona's fingers began to move in lazy strokes up and down his back. "Are you dead or alive?"

"Close to death, but not quite. Half-dead, maybe." Her love, his, made it difficult to move away.

"Your phone is ringing again. I was worried you would have stopped to answer it." He pulled back at her comment, glad to see the teasing look in her eyes. "It might have been more important."

"There isn't anything in the world more important than you in my bed."

She bit her lip. "What if it's Selena? I thought of that, too."

Cathal lifted himself off her and flipped to the bed beside her, his hands patting her thigh. "I can't imagine I'll be much use in that situation. But I'll check it now, seeing as it's ringing for the sixth time."

He climbed from the bed, grabbed his gym shorts, and walked to the bathroom first before grabbing his phone. Every inch of his body felt loose. Relaxed. It was the feeling he usually treasured and would push him into the rare sleep. Now, he could enjoy it knowing rest would come on its own.

Rian's number showed on the caller I.D., "Hello?"

"About damn time you heard your phone."

"I heard it before, you idiot, I was busy."

"Oh." The small sound of shock and maybe pride in his voice made Cathal smile. "I'm calling as you have a new niece on the way. We're headed to the hospital. Brogan took Selena."

"Alright. These things take time, right?"

"I'd say yes, and our Rosie might be as stubborn as the rest of us, but I'm more worried about someone being there for Brogan. He'd sounded a bit crazed on the phone with the way he was talking to himself, shouting me to get the car started-"

"Were you with him?"

"No. But Mara's ready to go now, so we'll see you there."

"Selena?" Fiona asked from the doorway to his room. He'd never invited a woman to his apartment, and he now appreciated the memory. Her standing there, bare-legged in his shirt, would be the only memory.

"Yes. She's already at the hospital. I need to go. I need to be there for Brogan and Rian." Because even if Rian didn't admit it, he needed the support as well.

She looked confused.

"I'll explain in the car. If you want to go?"

"Absolutely. Let me get changed." She paused beside him on the way to her room, kissing him wild and deep. "I enjoyed that."

"You sound shocked like you didn't think you would."

Fiona traced her finger along the edge of his jaw, loving the slight stubble. "Before you, I don't know if I ever have really enjoyed sex."

That was a difference he couldn't bring himself to point out. He had enjoyed sex before. But he'd never been driven to the edge of insanity by a woman before. Everything about her pushed him there.

He patted her bottom. "I'm going to grab a quick shower, and then we can leave." And he'd try to pull himself together. Sex had always been carefree, with no strings attached. Not with Fiona. He was bound to the woman it seemed. At the notion he'd walk away from her, his soul ached.

She padded to her room, his shirt barely covering her rear.

He ran a hand over his hair. He'd take a very, very cold shower.

20

The O'Keeley's had become like family to Fiona. That meant she stayed by Cathal's side throughout Selena's eleven-hour labor. Cathal had explained Rian's history in a matter-of-fact tone of voice on the ride to the hospital. But once they'd arrived, she'd spotted an unusual nervousness in Cathal. Jumpy. What Rian had gone through would upset the entire family.

Mara sat beside Rian, continually stroking a hand up and down his spine as they waited for news. Brogan had arrived in the waiting room, staying long enough to announce that little Rosie had made an appearance, before running back to Selena's side.

"Do you want to grab a bite to eat?" Fiona asked for the second time.

Cathal shook his head. He rested his elbows on his knees, leaned forward in the uncomfortable hospital waiting area. "I want to be here."

"Do you want me to go pick something up for you?" She raised her voice slightly. "Mara? Rian? Do you want anything to eat?"

Mara immediately looked at Rian.

He shook his head, still tense. The man hadn't spoken hardly two words since they'd arrived.

Cathal sat back and patted her knee. "But you need to go get something. I don't want you starving on our account."

"I'm fine." Her stomach chose that moment to rumble.

His lips twitched. "Go eat." He leaned to the side and pulled out his wallet, handing her a twenty.

"I can pay for my food."

The muscle in his jaw jumped. "I suddenly want you to bring me something back."

"You're a liar, but I'll bring something in hopes you will eat." She took the twenty and stood. "How about I bring us all something? That way, you can eat later, maybe."

Rian looked up and then at Mara. "That would be good. Do you want to go with her?"

"I will." She rose and ran a hand over Rian's hair. "Call me if you need me." She kissed him. "Rosie's alright. You heard Brogan say so."

Rian didn't respond.

Cathal's stood up and kissed Fiona's temple. "Thank you." He walked across the waiting room and sat down in the chair that Mara had vacated.

It was too easy to love him. He'd not responded when she'd told him, but that wasn't unexpected. He had so many walls, defenses built up around his future that he'd need time to absorb what it meant.

That she truly loved him.

Nothing he'd do would scare her away.

She met Mara in the hallway.

Mara kept her eyes cast downward. She covered her mouth as she yawned. "Sorry."

"No need to apologize, I think we're all exhausted after

not sleeping. Not that I can complain. Selena just stayed up all night *and* gave birth." Fiona pressed the down arrow for the elevator. "How's Rian holding up?"

Mara shrugged. "About as well as he seems. Tense. Nervous. Scared like hell. He'll get through it, though. They all will. How's Cathal?"

"I suspect he's more upset about Rian than anything." His eyes had watched Rian the majority of the night.

A small smile tilted Mara's lips up on one side. "Rian told me about you and Cathal."

"I assumed it wouldn't stay a secret long in this family." But she wasn't embarrassed. "Earlier, I told him I loved him."

Mara nodded and stepped onto the elevator. "Obviously, that didn't scare him away."

"No." And even though he'd said nothing in return, she knew he cared for her. Otherwise, she wouldn't have taken the risk.

"I was scared once that Rian would walk away instead of face down his issues." Mara walked peacefully beside Fiona as they exited the elevator and headed to the nearest fast-food restaurant in the hospital. "It took him a few days, but he finally figured it out. I know Cathal isn't Rian, and Rian told me about what happened to him. That has to be hard for him to live with."

Talking to someone about it might be a betrayal to Cathal, but Mara was family. Plus, Rian seemed just as stubborn so maybe Mara had some insight into how the brothers worked.

"I just want him to realize that I'm not going anywhere. No matter what."

Mara stopped at the back of the line at the fast-food

counter, sliding her hands into her back pockets. "Even if he loses control and seriously hurts someone?"

"No," she said without an ounce of hesitation. "Because I know what kind of man he is. But he won't believe me if I tell him that. He tried to break-up with me."

Mara didn't look shocked. She sighed. "He sounds as hardheaded as Rian."

Fiona ordered hers and Cathal's food. Mara did the same for her and Rian.

"I don't even know if they'll eat this." Fiona held the bag up. "It smells delicious." They walked back to the waiting room, but it was empty.

A nurse passed by. "The gentlemen asked me to tell you they went back to see their sister."

"Can we go?" Mara asked, already moving that direction. "Sure."

Fiona followed Mara down the hall. The deep sounds of laughter floated into the hallway.

Walking into the room, seeing their family together, solidified how much she was willing to fight for Cathal. Whatever he needed.

He stood beside the bed, holding his niece, with such a proud, shocked expression. A tear tracked down her cheek before she knew it.

A glance at Mara confirmed the woman had the same reaction. But her gaze remained locked on Rian. His entire demeanor had changed. Little Rosie held onto Rian's finger like she'd never let go.

Selena wiggled her fingers. "The boys said you went and bought them food. I sent Brogan to replace it so I can eat theirs. I'm *starving!*"

Fiona blinked, wiped her other cheek, and set the bag down on the table. "I have a cheeseburger or hamburger."

"I have chicken nuggets or a cheeseburger," Mara added.

Selena winced. "Can I have both the cheeseburgers?"

The two women laughed. "Absolutely," Fiona said. She took both the cheeseburgers to Selena. "Here. I can bet you worked up an appetite."

"Oh, yes. Rosie O'Keeley takes after every male in her family. Stubborn." She sighed. "And perfect."

"And good looking, just like her Uncle Cathal," Cathal murmured, causing everyone to laugh. His gaze met Fiona's, so open and happy. Not a trace of the shadows she'd seen last night.

Rian moved the little hand up and down, shaking his head. "You're prettier than he is."

Brogan moved into the room, carrying a bag of food, his eyes tired but alert. His brow relaxed when he spotted Selena eating. "How are you feeling?"

She chewed for a moment before swallowing. "The same way I felt five minutes ago when you left."

Rosie started to whimper and then let out an ear-piercing cry.

Both Rian and Cathal straightened. "Here." Cathal held her out to Brogan. "I didn't do it."

"Babies cry," Mara said, holding her arms out. Brogan kissed Rosie's pert nose before passing her off.

Mara grinned. "Oh, she is beautiful, Selena." She nudged Brogan with her elbow. "Y'all make pretty babies."

"Thank you. I'm partial to her." Brogan leaned over, watching his daughter's face as she settled down and stopped crying.

Cathal and Rian both reached for the fast-food bag.

"Now, you two are hungry." Fiona crossed her arms as she watched them each bite into a hamburger.

Rosie started to whimper again.

Fiona held her arms out. "I'm guessing Rosie's probably hungry as well, but I'd like a turn if you don't mind." She held her hands up. "I sanitized a few minutes ago."

Selena mumbled something through the large bite of the second cheeseburger.

Brogan laughed. "I think she said it was okay."

Fiona took the baby from Mara. Tiny little features. A perfect little nose. Her chin resembled Brogan's with a slight dip in the center. She found her fist, gumming it with her mouth.

The blanket was white, and the little outfit she wore was bubblegum pink with tiny green hearts all over it. She'd never contemplated kids. She and Hugo had never even discussed it.

She stroked a finger across the peach fuzz on Rosie's head. But did she want a baby?

Cathal watched her with an unreadable expression. Odd since she could typically sense his emotions so easily.

Rosie finally figured out her hand didn't have anything to eat and began to wail again. "Alright, your mama is done eating, so it's your turn." Fiona passed her off to Brogan. "She really is precious."

He smiled before handing her to Selena.

Selena reached for the top of her nightgown.

All at once, both Cathal and Rian let out a panicked, low volume scream.

"Wait!" Cathal took two steps before reaching back for the fast-food bag that contained the French fries.

Rian covered his eyes and stumbled toward the door where Mara caught him and ushered him out.

Cathal kept a hand up beside his face, blocking out the bed. "You gotta warn a man, Selena."

Selena chuckled. "I will."

Fiona followed Cathal out the door, quietly shutting it behind her.

"That was close. I love Selena, and whereas I know she's not my blood sister, that's one thing I just don't need to see. Brogan would gouge our eyes out."

She bumped shoulders with him. "Well, you're safe now. Are you sticking around or going home?"

He snagged a fry from the bag. "What are you doing?"

"Home. I need some sleep to run the bar till closing."

"Then I'm home with you. I'll swing back here to see them again before going into work. We've put Katie in charge for the time being." He draped an arm over her shoulder, pulling her tight. "Rosie O'Keeley." He shook his head. "Can't believe it. Ma would have loved her." He took a breath, a little shaky when he exhaled. "She'd have loved you, too."

She rubbed a hand up and down his back. "I'm sure I would have liked her as well. Any woman that could raise the three of you has to be amazing."

"She was that." They walked to his car in silence, leaving Rian and Mara at the hospital. She gave him his headspace to process the day. The deep v in his forehead finally smoothed out by the time they walked into his apartment.

She walked toward her room.

He picked her up, cradling her against his chest. "Nope."

"What?" She held onto his shoulders; the muscles were tight. "I told you..." She trailed off as it dawned on her. "Oh."

"Don't sound too excited." He dumped her in the middle of his bed. She bounced, laughing. He pulled off his T-shirt and tossed it on the floor. "From now on, I think you need to sleep in here. Bigger bed."

She smirked, glad the shadows from before had

disappeared. "And what, exactly, do you think we need a bigger bed for?"

Mischief gleamed in his blue eyes. "If you don't know, then I guess I'll need to demonstrate."

21

Cathal slipped out of bed and checked his phone. It was a quarter till eight. Fiona still slept, her wild red hair stretched out across her pillow. Her bare shoulder a reminder of how little she wore and how much he wanted to crawl back into bed beside her.

His phone showed a picture of Brogan, asleep in the glider rocking chair in Rosie's nursery, at three a.m. Little Rosie was nestled in the crook of his arm. Selena wrote: *Only way she would go to sleep.*

After the last five days since Rosie's birth, Cathal had not heard one complaint from his brother. Only small grumblings about dealing with boys when Rosie started dating. Cathal had laughed until he thought of himself at fifteen. Then he agreed with Brogan.

Cathal closed the door to the bathroom quietly and started the shower. He had an eight-thirty appointment with the prosecuting attorney for the lawsuit against O'Keeley's. He'd agreed to meet with him to figure out what direction the man was headed. What did he exactly want for his client? If he could get an angle on that, then he'd have a better idea what type of defense he'd mount.

And whether or not he'd take the fall.

Because now he knew he wouldn't have a choice. Not with Rosie here. Selena was a strong woman, but he'd do everything in his power to keep this stress from her. And Brogan.

A quick shave and he left the bathroom and walked into his closet. He'd never get used to his room being clean. The thought made him glance over at Fiona. Seeing her, holding Rosie, solidified that she belonged with someone better than him. God, it'd hurt like hell to watch her leave.

He dressed in his suit and slipped out of the apartment. The temperatures were heating up as summer moved into Atlanta. He didn't miss the oppressive heat.

The walk to the law firm took fifteen minutes, and by the time he arrived, he was ready. Thoughts of Rosie, Selena, and Fiona were shoved into a tight little box in the corner of his mind. A clear head was a necessity.

"I'm here to meet with Keith Winters." Cathal smiled at the receptionist.

The pencil she was wiggling between her fingers flew out of her fingers to the edge of the desk. "Yes, sir. Are you Mr. O'Keeley?"

"Yes."

"Just a moment." She reached for the phone and bumped her coffee. It sloshed over the edge, and she quickly wiped it up. "Darn!"

"Mr. O'Keeley?" A deep male voice called from the edge of a hallway to his left. "I'm Keith Winters."

Cathal ambled across the floor, not rushing or appearing nervous, and held out his hand. "Hi. You can call me Cathal."

"Keith. Well—" he held out his arm "-shall we get started? I hadn't expected your phone call." He walked ahead of Cathal down the long, nondescript hallway. Dark gray walls, light gray carpet. White trim. It curved slightly as they continued. He glanced into small offices on either side. Busy workers, heads down, typing away.

The life he'd leave behind.

He rubbed a finger over his lip to keep from smiling. He never really took to that workstyle anyway.

"We'll meet in here," Keith said, waiting for Cathal to pass before closing the door. "Like I said, I didn't expect to hear from you."

"Well, I'm just trying to figure out a few of the details. With this being virtually uncharted territory, I'm hoping that we can all come to an agreement."

"Not to put us off on a bad footing, but my client isn't willing to drop the charges."

"Oh, I hadn't expected him to." Cathal sat down in the high-backed leather chair, leaning forward with his hands clasped on the table. "But what exactly is he looking for? Aside from money."

"Accountability."

"Of the restaurant."

"He'd first wanted to find out the exact bartender who'd served the man. That's why we requested the video footage." Keith's eyes narrowed. "And you didn't have any."

Right. And he'd take the fall before he let the man know Selena was ultimately responsible.

"We have surveillance on the bars, but it doesn't extend back that far." Cathal smiled easily, laying his hands flat on the table. "I've actually been questioning that night myself as I work behind the bar when needed."

"Really?"

Cathal could see the money signs in Keith's eyes.

"Aside from accountability, the man has to have an ultimate goal. I know an amount was placed on the lawsuit, but what does it cover?"

"Future pain and suffering."

"Is he suffering?"

Keith jerked back under the pretense of being offended. "He was hit by a car. Yes, he is. He has extensive medical costs as the man who hit him didn't have insurance."

Cathal held up his hands. "Alright. But you'd ask the same question in my situation."

"Right. And if we had the video, we'd go after the server. You know it can carry criminal charges."

Yes. Cathal did know. But the bartender must be found negligent. Selena wasn't. And, at this point, if they did produce the video, he'd end up in jail regardless of hiding it.

He rose and held out his hand. "Thanks. You've helped. We're just trying to do what's fair to everyone involved."

Keith nodded and shook his hand. "I understand. I heard a rumor you left the firm you were with." He slipped his hand into his pocket and produced a business card. "If you're interested in working here, give me a call."

Cathal took the card with no intention of calling. He'd made up his mind. He didn't want to work on lawsuits, divorce cases, criminal cases...nothing. Nothing aside from maybe boring intellectual property rights would keep his anger in check.

He left but didn't return to his apartment. He slipped into the parking garage and climbed into his car. He had another stop to make.

Fiona's dad.

Mr. Grant wasn't expecting him, and that was probably for the best. Keith Winters had confirmed that either

O'Keeley's is held accountable or else Cathal faces potential criminal charges. His brothers didn't need the bad publicity. They didn't need a judgment handed down that painted them in a negative light. Their business was successful. Rian had changed his life to make sure the food was up to his standards. Brogan's entire life depended on O'Keeley's. With his wife and child at home, Brog didn't need the restaurant suffering for something like this.

That left Cathal.

He had no responsibilities. Nothing to ruin by going to jail if necessary.

He pulled into rush hour traffic on the I-75/85 Connector. Stop and go as usual. He usually hated traffic, but he'd take it for the moment. Because he needed to formulate what he'd say to Mr. Grant.

Fiona was his only regret.

She wasn't his wife, but he needed to have the situation with her da and the bar resolved. He could do that for her before possibly walking into a jail sentence next week.

The usual thirty-minute drive took fifty before he stepped out at Mr. Grant's business.

Cathal watched his reflection as he approached the doors to the Grant's headquarters, the mirrored window reflecting the confident set to his body.

He was determined. He'd meet with Mr. Grant, even if he had to wait for the man to leave work.

The security guard at the front took Cathal in from his shoes up. Cathal relaxed his posture and tried for a smile. "I'm here to see Mr. Grant."

"Please sign in." He stood and handed Cathal a pen. "What time is your appointment?"

"I don't have one."

The man's eyebrows rose. "Mr. Grant doesn't meet with anyone without an appointment."

"Can you let him know that Cathal O'Keeley is here?"

"I'll need to know a general idea of your business." The security guard shook his head. "Although not even that will get you an appointment."

"His daughter, Fiona, and I are living together." Cathal barred his teeth in something, not quite a smile. "I think he'll see me."

"Ah. I see." The security guard smirked. "I'll probably try not to alert Hugo that you're here. Not sure he's ever gotten over losing Fiona."

"Unless you're bored and want to break up a fight, then no, I don't suppose you should let him know."

The security guard chuckled. "I can imagine how that will turn out." He lowered his voice. "Although, between the two of us, I'd like to see it. Just not when I'm responsible."

Cathal nodded once. "I'll wait here."

The security guard dialed a number and waited a moment. "Mr. Grant has a visitor. Yes, I know the protocol, but I think he'd like to see this gentleman. Is he busy? Can you put me through? Yes, Sheila, I want to speak with Mr. Grant directly." He sighed and pinched the bridge of his nose. "Yes, I'm sure."

Cathal crossed his arms and leaned against the marbled wall, waiting.

"Mr. Grant? Hi, it's Bruce. Yes, sorry, but I didn't want Sheila to announce this. Cathal O'Keeley-" Bruce's eyes widened. "Yes. I'll have him wait here." He set the receiver down and cleared his throat. "He's on his way."

Cathal didn't move. "Thanks."

The door at the end of the hallway opened. Mr. Grant

stepped through, his hatred aimed directly at Cathal. He pushed the door open to the front of the building.

"Follow me," he said in a low voice, not waiting for a response.

"Alright." He walked out behind Fiona's father, squinting as the angle of the sun hit him.

Mr. Grant stopped a few feet away in the shade. "Why did you come here?"

"Because I wanted to speak to you about Fiona."

"I don't have anything to say to you or her." He crossed his arms and tilted his chin up. "This is a waste of my time."

"Since when is a discussion about a man's daughter a waste of time?"

"If you're here to ask for her hand in marriage, you can forget about my approval."

Cathal barked out a laugh. "I'd only ask for the permission of a girl's da if she needed it. Last I checked, your daughter does what she wants. I'm here because I wanted to ask you to back off on trying to get her bar shut down."

"You don't tell me-"

"How to parent? No. I'm certain you've messed that up on your own. My angle is more toward her future. You can't change the past, but you can stop all your plays from trying and having her business shut down. I hope by now you've realized she's not coming back to Hugo."

Mr. Grant's shoulders relaxed a fraction, but his eyes remained locked with Cathal's. "Yes. I have given that up after the display on my wife's birthday." He uncrossed his arms. "What's in this for you?"

"Just the security knowing that Fiona will be alright. I care for your daughter. I want her happy. I'd hope you'd want the same for her."

"Of course, I do. She could be happy back here, working alongside me."

Cathal rolled his shoulders, the tight feeling not easing. "Again, you've screwed that up yourself."

"Are you always this blunt?"

"No. But I don't have the time to dance around the subject at the moment." Because he had a week to make sure Fiona's future was secure before he walked away. "Because if you're not going to back off, then I have a few more stops to make." Cathal dropped his voice a notch. "I'm not playing around, Mr. Grant. I will make sure she's protected from you."

Mr. Grant paced away for a moment, hands casually resting on his hips, head tilted down. What was there to think about? If Cathal ever had a daughter, hell, simply being an uncle to Rosie made him want to do everything in his power to ensure she was happy.

Cathal gathered himself together to launch into another argument. But Mr. Grant turned. "I'm not doing this for you or me, but at the birthday party, I saw the hurt in her eyes. I know I didn't handle things the right way." He held out his hand. The first damn time the man initiated a handshake. "Thank you."

He sure as hell didn't expect that. "You're welcome, although I'm not sure what for."

"For being there for Fiona when we couldn't. She may never fully forgive me, but I'd like to at least make peace with her for now."

"Then I'll let you do that. I won't mention this to her if you don't mention I came to visit."

"So, she doesn't know about this?" Mr. Grant appeared shocked.

Cathal took his car keys from his pocket. "No. She

doesn't. She's just as determined a businesswoman as her father is."

His lips almost smiled. "I suppose she is."

A weight lifted off Cathal's shoulders. Fiona would be alright. "I'm going to let you get back to it."

Mr. Grant stepped toward the office building. "Her bar opens at three?"

"Yes." Cathal paused, watching Mr. Grant as he walked away. He didn't elaborate, but Cathal hoped he'd pay her a visit soon enough.

He sat down in his car and started the engine, debating on which way to go. It was nearly ten-thirty. Back to Fiona or the restaurant.

Neither. He grinned, thinking of another girl he needed to charm a few smiles from. Rosie.

22

T he bar was peaceful in the afternoon. Even with the way her life had turned upside down over the past few weeks, everything that'd happened with Cathal, the simple task of cleaning the counters, freezers, also brought Zen-like feelings to her world.

"Not busy, I see."

Her dad's voice stopped her cold. There went the Zen. "Dad, hi. What are you doing here?"

He sat down as if it were a regular occurrence. "I thought I'd have a beer."

If her eyes weren't attached to her brain, they'd have fallen out. "Excuse me? Since when you drink beer?"

"I happen to like beer." He knocked on the bar top. "I'm a paying customer now. Do you need to see my license to make sure I'm legal?"

Jokes? She couldn't help it. She glanced outside.

"Waiting for someone?"

"I'm making sure Hell hasn't frozen over, and there aren't pigs flying around." She pulled a frozen mug from the cooler and flipped the tap on the beer. "Did Hugo not want to make the trek with you?"

He waited until she handed him the drink. He took a small sip. "I didn't invite him."

She leaned on the bar and waited. She had a million things she could say to him, but she'd keep them all inside to know what was running through his head. His expression shifted between relaxed and confident to uncomfortable.

"Fiona, I came here to apologize." He didn't make eye contact, but the words hit her harder than anything else he could've said. "I promised I wouldn't say anything, but I think you should know that Cathal came and visited me today."

She was wrong. That shocked her more. "When? I thought he was in a meeting all morning."

"A few hours ago. He was trying to make sure that you and your bar would be alright. Made it seem as though he was leaving."

Leaving. *What the hell, Cathal?*

"I see." She didn't, at all, but she'd deal with Cathal later.

"I don't think you do. Although I might not have been directly responsible for turning in your bar, Hugo did. And I allowed it. I'd hoped that if you lost the bar, you'd have no choice but to come home. And I didn't care at the time if it made you angry." He drank deeply from his glass, setting it down half-empty. "Your anger I could handle. But at your mother's birthday party, I saw the hurt. I watched you walk out the door, and it finally dawned on me that this was it. That'd I'd pushed so hard that you were leaving. I...I don't want that, Fiona."

"I'm not coming back to work for you. I don't want to do that for a living, and I definitely don't want to work with Hugo."

"I know." He slouched on the chair, looking like so many others that'd come into her bar with the world pressing down on their shoulders. But he was her dad. "I don't expect you to come back to the business. But I want to invest in your bar."

She glanced around. Nope. Nothing around them had burst into flames with his statement. "That's the last thing I'd thought you'd ever say to me."

"It's taken far too long to say it."

"But I don't want your money, Dad."

He sighed and finished the beer in another large swallow. "I figured you'd decline the offer. I would've as well."

"But you can come in, have a beer after work sometime. I'd like that."

His gaze met hers. He nodded once. "I'd like that, too."

A female's voice drifted into the bar a second before Katie walked through the door, her phone on her ear and talking a mile a minute. She waved at Fiona and then held up one finger.

"I know you have a business to run, so I'll let you do that." He pulled out a ten-dollar bill.

"You don't have—"

"I do." He set it down and patted it. "I'm a paying customer, after all." He started to leave but paused. "I know your mother would like to see you."

"I can come by for Sunday lunch like I used to."

His smile was tentative but still there. "I'd like that."

Fiona blinked, trying to clear away the tears as he left the bar. Damn, Cathal. Why had he gone and rescued her again? Because she always hated the Superman routine in a man. But that was before him. He'd been the only person in the world to have her back. Support her. And he wanted to leave. Not for any real reason. No. She knew that much. He would walk out of her life because of the twisted-up thoughts inside his head.

"Hi!" Katie ducked underneath the bar and held her arms open.

Eventually, Fiona might get used to all the hugs. "This is a surprise. Aren't you supposed to be at O'Keeley's?"

"Yes, but Cathal is covering for me while I came down to talk to you."

"Why?"

"I want a job. At night. I really enjoyed working here while you were gone. And Cathal said you sometimes have a major crush at the door." She swiveled her head around, surveying the space. Her blond hair with neon green tips swayed with the motion. "I really dig this place. Always have."

Cathal strikes again. "Katie, you don't have to do this. I don't know what Cathal said—"

"Said?" Katie half-laughed. "Nothing. That man doesn't have to say a word for us all to know how much he loves you. I asked where you were today, and he said here. He *might* have put the idea in my head, but this is all me. I want to do this, Fiona. If you can't pay me—"

"No. I can pay you. And it would be nice to have someone to help. It'll keep me from having to get the security guard to watch the bar while I run to the bathroom."

Katie tilted her head to the side. "I wondered about that when I worked the bar. But what do you say?" She held her arms out. "I'm yours if you want me."

Fiona took a solid breath. "Yes. I'd like that."

"Great!" She did a little dance in a circle. "Can I start tonight?"

"I need you to start tonight. I need to go wrestle a bossy Irishman in a couple hours."

Katie's eyes lit up. "Oh? Are you against giving a girl details?"

"Not that kind of wrestling."

"Oh. Too bad. I hope it doesn't make things weird, but I may have a small infatuation with your boyfriend. But don't worry," she held her hands up, "I'm strictly in the audience admiring him from afar."

Fiona laughed and reached for her water. "I don't blame you." But she was in love with Cathal for an entirely different reason. And it was time to make sure he knew she wouldn't walk away. No matter what happened, what he did, she'd be by his side.

It was a risk. A big one. But she wouldn't let him throw what they had away. It was time for him to understand that.

She worked behind her bar until nearly eight, when she'd planned for Katie so show up. After a few additional administrative items, she left.

As she approached the apartment, she heard low voices inside. Odd. Cathal said he never brought anyone to his place.

Her hand raised to knock, but she pulled it back down. She tried the knob, and it was unlocked.

The voices stopped as she entered. All three brothers, along with little Rosie in Brogan's arms, stood in his living room. They watched her, no one speaking for a few moments. Cathal seemed to come alive first.

"You're home?"

That wasn't the welcome she'd wanted, but judging by the intense expressions of the men, she'd take it as literal as possible.

"Yup. Katie is officially an employee. I wanted to talk to

you about that. That's why I came home early." She gave Brogan and Rian a small wave. "But I can see you're busy."

Disappointment flashed in his eyes. "Yes. We are in the middle of something about the restaurant."

Fiona held her arms out. "Here. Let me take Rosie into the bedroom and close the door, and you guys can finish up."

Rian looked a little surprised.

Brogan looked relieved.

Cathal still watched her with a strange mix of emotions. Something battled in his mind. She wanted to know what it was, but he'd have to come to her with it. She'd be there. No matter what. That vow she made to herself wouldn't be broken.

Brogan passed Rosie off. "I appreciate it. But fair warning, she somehow knows when I sit down. I haven't gotten her to sleep anywhere other than in my arms *while* I'm standing since seven this morning."

"I'm up for the challenge. Sit. Take a load off." She swayed gently with Rosie as she started to wake up. "I don't know how you're going to stand to have such a pretty daughter, Brogan."

He ran a hand over his head and practically fell back into Cathal's sofa. "Me neither to tell you the truth."

She stepped to Cathal, raised her face, and kissed him quickly before he could respond. Something was up if he'd let her get away with such a short greeting.

"Rosie and I are going to have girl time." She picked up her diaper bag and then stepped confidently to Cathal's room.

Not hers.

She turned to shut the door. Confusion remained on

Cathal's face. Brogan's eyes were closed. Rian hadn't said a word, but he was watching Cathal, not her.

Everyone had rallied around Cathal. Did he see that?

She closed the door and set the bag on the edge of the bed. "Now, pretty Rosie, let's see how long it takes your uncle to realize I'm not leaving."

23

C athal sat in the back of the courtroom, oddly calm, considering he was about to take the fall for the restaurant and, most of all, for Selena. It was for all of them. Except for Fiona. She'd ended up collateral damage, and that was the last thing he'd ever wanted.

He'd tried again early this morning to break things off, but she kept sidestepping the subject. She could be more persuasive than even the best lawyers in the shower at six a.m.

Now his redhead sat beside him, her hand resting on his knee, completely unaware of the storm. Calm. Confident. It was safer if she didn't know. Brogan and Rian wouldn't think twice about lying to keep Selena safe. Selena, Fiona, and Mara, at least, could deny knowledge.

Fiona squeezed his knee. "Why do you look so tense? I thought you already agreed with your brothers to a partial settlement. I don't see how they could charge any of the bartenders with negligence. They don't have proof that anyone had any knowledge that the man became intoxicated at O'Keeley's or was already drunk when he showed up."

Cathal shrugged, his suit jacket too tight. "Never know how these things will go."

Her gaze remained on his profile. He felt it. She'd always been able to read him, and right that moment, he hated it. For her. The secret between them turned his stomach sour.

Or was that the mere thought of walking away?

"Why don't you go ahead and go to your bar? This might take a while."

She kissed his cheek. "Nice try. You're not getting rid of me that easy. You're hiding something."

He closed his eyes. If they decided to press charges directly against him, his law career was over. Not that it mattered since he planned on quitting.

There's no way the prosecutor wouldn't bring his prior history into his argument to discredit him. And Fiona would be guilty by association. By being in a relationship with a murderer.

His gut twisted again. "Leave, Fiona," he said with a little more force. I'm serious."

"Which is why I'm staying." She crossed her arms and sat back.

"Stubborn," he mumbled.

"Hard-headed."

"You don't need to be with me." He looked at his hands, flexing his fingers open and closed. "I told you that in the beginning. I think our relationship has run its course." The words barely made it past his lips.

She set her hand over both of his. "Stop it. I know what you said, and I've told you once before that I loved you. That means every dirty part of your past."

"You shouldn't."

"It's a good thing that I don't listen to you." She huffed. "I love being with you. With your family. At the restaurant. I feel more a part of your family than my own. Don't push me away because you think it's for my own good." She cupped his cheek, turning his face to hers.

How did this woman care so much for him? He could see it. She meant every word she said.

"Talk to me, Cathal. What's really going on?"

He let out a ragged breath. She'd find out soon enough. He shifted closer, lowering his voice. "We found the video of that night. Of who served the guy."

Her eyes widened. She didn't call him on lying about the tape, which encouraged him.

"Selena."

Fiona's lips parted. "No."

"And since I'm the one with the least amount to lose..."

Fiona was smart. "Shit." She'd figured it out. Maybe now she'd walk away.

The judge called for the parties in the O'Keeley's Irish Pub to come forward. Fiona kissed his lips before he could move. She leaned her forehead against his. "Not anymore, Cathal. No matter what happens, you have to know I love you. I'm not going anywhere. Ever. Even if you take the brunt of this, I'll be here."

She meant it. Her blue fairy eyes held his, so fierce and determined like she was ready for whatever fight he wanted to mount.

"Mr. O'Keeley?" The judge called again.

"Figure out something else. You're the smartest person I know." She gave him a lopsided smile. "You managed to make me fall in love with you. If you want to take care of me, I don't need you to talk to my dad or Katie; I need you. I need you to fight for us."

He swallowed over the lump in his throat. God, he loved his woman.

He walked forward to the judge, his mind racing between what he'd say and Fiona. She shouldn't love him. He'd killed a man. He could hardly control himself or his anger at times. He didn't deserve it. Yet, there she sat, in the back of the courtroom, arms crossed, her chin tilted up with that fiery expression.

Loving her in return was easy. He'd done that for the past few weeks. Probably months. But accepting her love meant putting her at risk. It was easier to be alone, not have anyone else depending on him if he screwed up. Lost control.

The judge, a woman with jet black hair and porcelain skin, had asked him a question.

"I'm sorry, can you repeat that?" Cathal slipped his hands into his pockets, focusing on the judge who already looked exasperated.

"I said that you called for this summary judgment. What is your plea?"

"O'Keeley's..." He looked back at Fiona. He thought of Selena. He'd still make sure she wasn't implicated.

But for the first time in fifteen years, he wanted a future. He wanted Fiona for himself. He'd fight.

That meant he'd have to do what he thought was right.

"O'Keeley's wants to accept partial responsibility." The murmur through the courtroom confirmed that no one had expected that.

"Partial? And what does that entail?" asked the judge.

Keith Winter, the other lawyer, stood beside him, watching Cathal with a curious expression.

"We don't feel as though we purposefully or negligently over-served anyone. But, after review of our records, the night listed in this lawsuit meant I was behind the bar at some point."

"Did you serve the individual in question?" The judge raised an eyebrow. "Or was anyone else serving that night?"

"I can't remember." That lie was for Selena. And Brogan. "But you need to realize that we operate a family restaurant. We don't even have televisions behind the bar. It's not a gathering place that becomes overcrowded as other bars might. If anyone were acting intoxicated, they would have been asked to leave. I have no memory of serving the individual or to him being drunk."

"So, you can't answer if you served him?" The judge raised her eyebrows.

Cathal stilled his body. "No. I can't. But I'd like to propose a settlement."

"I haven't seen the terms," Keith chimed in before the judge could respond. "I do not agree to anything."

"We offer to cover the plaintiff's medical bills that are not covered by his insurance for the next two years for all injuries related to the accident."

The lawyer had asked for a flat settlement, one price for pain and suffering. Cathal knew his offer was better. Plus, O'Keeley's wouldn't have to fork out all the money at once.

The judge sat back. "And that is your offer when you don't think you're guilty?"

"Correct. We hate that our establishment is at all linked to this. We'd like the charges dismissed, and we'll enter into a private arrangement with the individual."

Keith walked back to the table to speak with the other lawyer and the plaintiff.

Fiona sat forward in her seat, her eyes glued to his.

He winked.

She smiled, his entire body instantly relaxing. That was

the woman he wanted for the rest of his life. He'd never thought he'd find her. Never wanted it.

"Mr. O'Keeley?" The judge looked impatient again. "Are you with us?"

Cathal smiled up at the judge. "Sorry again."

She gave him a stern look. "I'd appreciate you paying attention."

Keith approached the bench. "My client accepts the conditions." He cut his eyes at Cathal. "He feels like it's more than adequate."

"Very well." The judge entered the motion to dismiss the case. "I'll let the parties privately determine the terms."

Cathal turned, shook Keith's hand, and then ambled back down the aisle. Brogan and Rian would just have to accept what he'd entered them into. He was prepared to take the fall, admit to the fault, keep the restaurant from being hit with *another* blow.

But Fiona changed that.

She waited for him by the door. "Done?"

"Not yet." He walked into her arms, slipping his hand behind her back to pull her close for a kiss. A long, thorough kiss that made the judge hit the gavel a few times to break them apart.

"Mr. O'Keeley!" The judge said with her voice raised, carrying through the courtroom.

Cathal put his arm around Fiona's shoulders and turned to face her. "Yes?"

"That's enough."

"It's not even close to enough, your Honor." Cathal led Fiona out the door and down the hallway.

Fiona leaned back, staring up at him. "What are you going to do now?"

"First, I'm going to tell you that I love you, too."

Surprise popped into her eyes. "I wondered if you'd say it in return. What's the second thing?"

He kissed her again, long enough that a few people passing by cleared their throat. He lifted his head, cupping her face in his hands. "Second, I'm going to do my best to convince you to marry me."

Fiona's lips parted. "Marry you?"

"Today." He grinned. "We are at a courthouse after all."

EPILOGUE

"A re you sure you don't mind us coming along on your honeymoon?" Selena swayed gently, holding Rosie against her chest. Finally, the teething child had gone to sleep. Her first international trip and the little thing decided to cut her first tooth. Selena nuzzled her sweet-smelling hair. "I assumed that you'd like time alone with Cathal."

Fiona rocked in the chair, her head tilted back, her eyes closed. "I'd rather have you all here. We're going to fly to Paris for a couple days before going back home, but I wanted to come here, bring Cathal back, with his brothers." She opened her eyes and looked at Selena. "And not that I don't love your men, but if you left me alone with the three of them for a week, someone might not survive."

Mara laughed, rocking in a chair right beside Fiona. "I'd place my money on the two of them turning on Rian first. I love my man, but he has a serious, personal vendetta against certain food."

Selena gazed out at the view. They'd rented a cottage off the Dingle Peninsula on Great Blasket Island. Gorgeous views with green hills, blue skies, and isolation for the six of them, and Rosie, to be together. Life with O'Keeley's Pub made downtime as a family difficult to find. They'd had to travel across the ocean to Ireland to find a break from the rush of their daily lives.

"We need to promise to come back here every year." Fiona took a sip of wine. "Damn, but Rian knows how to pick out wine."

Mara nodded. "Yes, he does." She sighed, and both women looked at her. "If we come back next year, we may need to rent a larger house."

"No way," Selena said in the loudest voice possible without waking up Rosie. "But I thought Rian wouldn't have children." Selena had always hoped he'd change his mind, but she wouldn't push him. She'd almost ruined his relationship with Mara by doing that.

"We had a long talk when we took that walk yesterday." Mara's broad smile brought a smile to Selena's face. "He said being with Rosie for the week made him change his mind about kids."

Fiona barked out a laugh and then covered her mouth and sent Selena an apologetic look when Rosie whimpered. "Sorry. That's just funny seeing as Cathal being around a teething baby all week pushed him into stockpiling condoms. Apparently, we have a case arriving at the apartment when we get back."

Mara sat forward, clasping her hands together. "He's still scared about it, but he said that it was worth the risk to have Rosie, and he's willing to take the risk. We'll wait until after we get married in September, but the fact he's made that decision now is amazing."

Fiona leaned to the side and gave Mara a hug. "I'm happy for you."

"Me, too," Selena said.

Rosie let out a loud cry.

Fiona stood and held out her hands. "Here. My turn. You sit."

Selena passed her daughter to Fiona. "I had no idea that being a mom meant wanting your children with you every second of the day and wanting one second to yourself at the same time." Selena sat down, watching Fiona bounce Rosie until she stopped crying. "How's the construction of the new bar going?"

"Good." Fiona shifted Rosie, so she faced outward. Her cries quieted down. "Cathal has too many ideas to contain at this point. I had no idea he'd enjoy running the bar with me this much. He doesn't seem to miss working for the law firm at all."

"We both commented the other day about how happy he seemed." Mara looked back at the view of the Atlantic Ocean. Even from this distance, they could smell the saltwater. "He's settled. Rian's the same way. Everything that ate at them inside is at peace." She turned her gaze to Selena. "What about Brogan?"

"Not sure Brogan is ever at peace. The man hasn't worn a suit in a week or barked out orders, and I'm certain he's going through withdrawals. I almost brought a suit on the trip just so he could put it on in our room and walk around a little bit." Selena laughed along with the women. "Other than missing bossing people around, he seems to be doing really good right now. Rosie has loosened him up considerably. That and having both Rian and Cathal stable."

She spotted Brogan, walking up the hill toward the cottage. Rian and Cathal trailed behind. The man still made her heartbeat quicken. The conservative navy sweater and tan slacks contrasted to his dark hair, messing up as the wind blew across the hillside. He looked as wild as the ocean behind him.

Mara, still rocking a steady rhythm in her chair, asked, "Do you think we'll ever get used to it?"

"No." Fiona's quick response had the women laughing.

Brogan topped the hill, flanked on either side by his bothers. Rosie squealed and began kicking her legs, her chubby arms flailing out to the side.

Selena took Rosie from Fiona, setting her daughter's small body on her hip. Rosie let out another excited squeal. "Even our little Rosie knows what fine men she has watching out for her, and I plan to tell her that every chance I get."

The End

Made in the USA
Middletown, DE
15 September 2020

19907571R00130